# THE BRICK HOUSE

# THE BRICK HOUSE

MICHELINE AHARONIAN MARCOM

*Illuminations by Fowzia Karimi*

AWST
PRESS

*The Brick House*

© 2017 Micheline Aharonian Marcom

First Edition, First Printing, 2017

Awst Press
P.O. Box 49163
Austin, TX 78765-9163
awst-press.com
awst@awst-press.org

Printed in the United States of America

Distributed by Small Press Distribution

ISBN: 978-0-9971938-5-5

Library of Congress Control Number: 2017945982

Editing: Tatiana Ryckman
Copyediting: Emily Roberts
Book design: LK James

*Ah, ye admonitions and warnings! why stay ye not when ye come? But rather are ye predictions than warnings, ye shadows! Yet not so much predictions from without, as verifications of the foregoing things within. For with little external to constrain us, the innermost necessities in our being, these still drive us on.*

—Herman Melville, *Moby Dick*

*He understood that modeling the incoherent and vertiginous matter of which dreams are composed was the most difficult task that a man could undertake, even though he should penetrate all the enigmas of a superior and inferior order; much more difficult than weaving a rope out of sand or coining the faceless wind.*

—Jorge Luis Borges, "The Circular Ruins"

*It is not outside, it is inside: wholly within.*

—*Meister Eckhart*

*For Hank and for Karen,*

*friends who shared with me a way*


*For Fowzia,*

*who dreams the real*

# DREAM OF—

## 1

## 2

## 3

# 7

# THE BRICK HOUSE

※

THE BRICK HOUSE IS NOT like any other house on the moor. Here the land stretches out greenly with its allochthonous grasses and the house stands matronly and alone on a rise on the wild sedge like an ancient dynamo and one Sitka spruce and two pines lean in close to it as if to embrace the red brick or to shield it. In the distance, the green abruptly becomes the grey immutable line of the sea and just there an old lighthouse stands with its flashing lantern and it is toward this beacon that the dreamers will travel at night, fro and to the brick house, with a frightening, consolatory regularity.

The white tower is the only other abode for miles and it too has the neglected air of things which have become outmoded and unnecessary and of interest now, like a curio, mainly to small children and their mothers who might visit as they would a zoological garden to gawk at an obsolete (automated for twenty-three years) object of history. The former keeper and his wife and three children departed this outcropping more than two decades ago with their beaten-in valises and china cups and unbound, tattered nautical maps, and since that time the tower-house has been shut up and the premises abandoned. The fence around the building's perimeter now lies in ruins next to the manmade jetty whose enormous stones appear an unearthly bright jewel-green -orange -purple when wet, and upon drying, unmagical, humanly placed, and grey-colored.

To what end does a traveler journey to this remote peninsula? And how does he arrive to this place that, like a conch, holds the sound of water at its back? There is first a chance encounter with a stranger in an urban marketplace, and then several days later, a phone call late at night and the date and ferry schedule are given him to travel with his black suitcase and heavy top coat, brown boots, and woolen gloves. The sea is greyer in the hours before dusk when the traveler steps onto the gangway in his winter attire.

The caretaker awaits him at the entrance to the ferry terminal. She is old, although of an imprecise age, wrinkled and pale skinned, but underneath her unsunned pallor lie the manifold tribes the traveler is not certain he can determine, although he is certain they abide there. Antecedents with eyes from outer continents or this continent's aboriginal inhabitants must lurk inside her invisible bloodpool, he thinks, as she greets him with the usual decorous words in the passenger pickup area.

The caretaker directs him to put his valise inside the trunk and to climb into the car. He sits down next to her and he doesn't inquire if she is a tribal member from the cold northern regions of the white ice, or if she hails from the desiccated, hotter lowlands, the wet equatorial forests; perhaps there are fourteenth-century Near Eastern tattoos covering her arms and legs like a coded message, he thinks, but if so he cannot see them. They depart the terminal and turn onto the interstate and she tells him he will stay in a room she calls ex-eleven and that they will arrive just as the sun disappears beyond the sound. Afterwards she is silent. And it occurs to the traveler as they speed down the two-lane highway into the forest in the quiet gloaming of the late afternoon, how the races and fears and loves of tribes of men must be held in all of us and circulate, as cars circulate on North American thoroughfares, black-topped and well-lighted and free-seeming to each one who drives his car along their awfully predestined routes.

The caretaker shuts off the engine at the front entrance of the brick house and she steps down from the car. She doesn't offer assistance with his luggage (as she didn't offer her help at the ferry terminal) and she seems in fact annoyed now, as if he has put her out with his late-winter, late-afternoon reservation. But this annoyance, or another emotion, he is not sure which precisely, could merely be a product of his imagination, for he realizes that his heart is pounding a little faster and harder than usual as he approaches the front doors (so that he notices the invisible muscle's cadence, the strengths of its pressure in his chest), and his breaths are tight and shallow (so that he calculates that he should breathe, forcefully draws a long breath to the lower reaches of his lungs). Perhaps he only imagined it, he reasons with himself, concocted from his own fears the feeling that the caretaker was put out by his arrival today and then projected this emotion onto her body, like an old movie projector does the film reel onto a darkened white screen. The house had appeared quiet and massive and alone on the rise and an electrical light had shone in the vestibule as they approached it only moments ago. In a high room in the northwest corner of the building, an electrical light was also lighted, the sun no longer in the sky.

*Bathtowels have been put on the bed for your convenience*, the caretaker says, breaking her silence after he enters the building. *Bathe in the morning and afterwards remember to drink a glass of our water*, and she stresses the words *remember* and *our*. *It will refresh you*, she continues, as if some kind of old medicine resided inside of the fluid, as if the times hadn't either poisoned or added chlorine and fluoride or petrochemical residues to it, and perhaps they have not here on this distant outcropping. *Welcome*, she finishes, and he is not sure if he's been called—Well? Come—or given the phrase as usual and unthinkingly.

He follows the caretaker up the staircase to the second story and he sees a long hallway stretch out before him. There are seven doors in the corridor, three at the left and four at the right, and etched onto a brass plaque on each of these doors is a letter followed by a number, out of any kind of discernible (to him) order: X11 is second on the left from N49; and below each letter-number, a pictograph. The images look vaguely familiar to him, yet strange and exotic, as if having taken their inspiration from the tales of the immortal emperors and fantastic beasts told him during his childhood. He follows the caretaker to X11 and sees the unusual figure of a dragon and a man, the head and torso of the monster and the legs and sex of the man, and a strange sensation comes over him (the hairs stand up on the back of his neck) but he is not sure what exactly he feels, just as he doesn't know why this long and painted green-brown hallway (the hue of uncooked lentil seeds) with its seven doors and one electrical light at the far end makes him so nervous, as if he might lose himself inside of this building, as if he will not return or resume after he crosses the threshold to the room because the man that he is (that he thinks he is) might come apart or will not hold inside its walls? And he was taught, and he has learned, to mistrust, disregard, or unknow the things for which there is no logical, factual explanation, which is why he had decided to visit the brick house in the first place: for he had determined that a sojourn here could benefit him in some manner. He needed a vacation, he'd realized that day in the marketplace with the stranger, a break, a small breach with his life as he'd known it for decades. Now, however, as he stands at X11 he wishes that he were at home in his city with his wife and children and the various sundry habits he has filled his days with, including the conversations he might have had with his spouse about his cruel bosses and the rising costs of goods and petrol and news headlines and politics and the shameless divorcée next door and why friends are no longer loyal and which bills to pay in full and how many appointments with dentists this year and fixing the roof cutting the overgrown fruit trees cleaning up the garden paying notpaying paying the bills and collectors and more bills, retirement benefits, weekend social engagements, rising medical insurance premiums and—how happy and secure, he thinks, I could have been tonight if only I had refused the invitation.

The monster stands at attention on the bronze plate and the man uses the key the caretaker gave him and opens the solid rosewood door of X11. He enters the room and the caretaker has bidden him goodnight and forbidden the ingestion of medicines or alcohol for the inducement (or abetment) of sleep. This is one of three rules in the house: that those who visit must dream what their room proffers unburdened by outside stimulants or depressants. He was not surprised by the caretaker's directive, for the stranger had already explained the regulations to him when they spoke on the telephone at midnight one week ago.

*Remember,* the caretaker said before she turned her back and walked down the dimly lighted green-brown hallway toward the stairwell, *that you are not to enter into another dreamer's room and disturb her or the dream either.* This is the second admonition and like the other visitors who come to the brick house, he will not violate its laws for he knows that it is neither possible nor desirable to die anyone's death but his own.

✳

SHE NOTICED THE HALF-MOON IN the darkening blue sky on the drive from the ferry, although in her city ignorance she couldn't tell if the moon was waxing or waning, rising or setting. Her room is sparsely furnished. A bed big enough for one person is pushed up against a corner; a small antique bureau, old and chipped, stands against another wall; a cheap-looking nightstand with the plastic coating peeling off its top surface is to the right of the bed. There is a rusted metal night lamp; a polyester coverlet (large white roses on golden vines on a green background) on the bed; a small closet; the solid rosewood door. The room, like the hallway, is painted a desiccated green-brown, a shade of paint which, inexplicably to her, one often finds in state-run and military institutions. The furniture does not welcome her with its woodgrain or style; it sits heavily upon the floor as old stone monuments do, as if it has always been here, as if it were older even than its makers: silent, immutable, strong-willed. And enraged, she thinks, for she notices that the bureau glares at her in reproach and how the chipped nightstand is mean and beaten-looking and seems to beat her now, and *What have I done?* she asks herself again, and feels again her fear and unease. The night lamp refuses to look into her eyes and stares, instead, at the stained grey carpeting covering the old wooden floors; the invisible wooden floors crrk and shift beneath as she walks about the room.

*Tonight is the farthest away you will go*, the caretaker said lastly, after she had handed her the key.

She undresses self-consciously (ashamed of her naked form) and dons her nightdress quickly under the dark looks of bureau and nightstand. She lies on the bed and pulls the bedcovers to her chin. Her body is aging and the fat hangs at her upper arms and lower belly and thighs; her skin is dry and wrinkled around her eyes and loose at her knees and elbows. She knows that she is now knowing her own decay, she—a fifty-six-year-old woman in room B27—and *Goodnight*, she says to herself, to the bureau, nightstand, and closet, loudly. She shuts off the light and thinks that she should not have come here. That she will die. That she is lonely. That her former spouse did not love her, her children do not love her enough (her parents, aunts, friends). And a panic takes hold of her neck and she lies waiting, thinking that she will never sleep, that she cannot in unknown places and without a chemical aid of some kind or alcohol. Then she has opened her eyes and it is early morning. She rises and goes to the toilet and pisses loudly and brushes her teeth as usual, leaves the used bath towel on the floor against her personal habits of hygiene (following the instructions given yesterday by the caretaker), and drinks a glass of water from the tap with some trepidation.

# ONE

# THE KILLERS

*He who has not yet killed, shall kill. She who has not
yet given birth, shall bear.*

—Abyssinian song

R HAS TAKEN ANOTHER SIP of her wine and she has asked C if
he will fuck her tonight. She doesn't make her request by use of the
interrogative, however, but rather as a savage string of exclamations
and small shouts about other, unrelated subjects (credit card state-
ments, an unpaid mortgage, an unfixed fence and toilet, his job). C
sits at the dinner table across from R and tells her of the books on
his bedside table that need his attention, much like children need
to know the whereabouts of their mothers when they have become
lost in strange cavernous halls and marketplaces. He tells her of the
riotous god Dionysus (he recounted several legends of the Bacchic
mysteries to their daughters when the girls were small.) C insists he
loves only R and how the other women during their long marriage
were mere diversions from the main source of his love and his cock
inside the other cunts meant nothing, but the neglected books must
be attended to tonight, he says; therefore, she might be his lover
again tomorrow after he first decodes the strange texts.

R uses her hands to demonstrate how she prefers he stimulate her clitoris. Like this, she says, as she nestles the thumb between the index and second fingers of her left hand and with two fingers of her right, agitates the thumb's tip vigorously. She then picks up the serrated knife next to her dinner plate and seeks all of the blood she can release from C with her hands and the metal utensil.

A stranger enters the large and locked home on the hill and kills R. Now husband and wife lie supine on the floor. Now their heads are removed, and hands and feet, and the blood is red everywhere until a curtain can be pulled back like a lever to reveal the mystical writings in the black cuneiform script above their mutilated forms on the white dining room wall.

# THE TWIN

A MAN LOOKS INTO THE mirror. He is tired and he can hardly keep his eyes open. Look at this, he says to himself, and he begins: I woke earlier than usual today and I was surprised at my surroundings and that I was in fact here, or, rather, that I had returned unscathed to the brick house. And yet I was at home and my wife slept violently by my side. Had I dreamed the brick house? Or had it slyly, inventively inverted and then dreamed me in my city? My wife breathed heavily as if she were running. She was the kind of woman I had envisioned when I was an adolescent: the large, doughy water-colored eyes; the large, tidy fingers and polished fingernails; the efficacious sweeper and cleaner and keeper of the children. She upkept the norms and a schedule and decorum and she bored me like a schoolmaster bores his pupils. We were happy. And with her pointing index finger, red lacquered and tight, my wife ruled my days like God ruled Adam.

The girl who awaited me with open-legged invitation (my wife clenched her buttocks, her sex, and cleaned my sons' foreskins and forbade them to "play" (as she put it) with their unseemly appendages) swam in the fetid waters of my nightmares. She pushed aside the floating plastic bottles and black polyethylene bags with her teeth; she consumed the petroleum sludge like an afternoon soda; she made sexual circuits with the bloated, mercury-filled flesh of large fish and whales who accompanied her nighttime walks in the deep, polluted, and dying sea waters of the Pacific.

I was on an island in the vast and awful, blue like a dome, exquisite, and gloomy sea. The trade winds blew almost continuously so that the tall, spindly palms leaned into the air and embodied the invisible airworld with its powerful currents (much like marionettes express the manipulations of the unseen puppeteer's hands) via their forms. (And when on rare occasion the wind did not rise, three or four palms remained loyal partisans to the air, unable to return to the upright stand of the seaside gallery of trees.) Norfolk pines stood guard like erect green sentries on the inland roads.

Then I am traveling the seas on a whaler and my eldest son stands near me with the heavy ropes coiled around his not-knees, for he has no face or body, only his voice stands inside of the circle of hemp, only his name. The dead, clean-looking, blue sea stretches out toward the lighter blue sky where they converge at a black line inside my mind. A female humpback breaches in front of the ship and my son laughs to see it. A calf mimics the female forthwith in a smaller breach following the silent instructions from its mother below the canopy of wild water with a tail flip or God knows how she instructs her brood. Another breach by the white monster and I am terrified and God pushes his finger into my chest and I fall back onto my son and He pushed us both flat onto the wooden deck and I have ruined him. The mother whale climbs aboard the ship and inches toward me; unmysterious now, fat and awkward, her teats spray gallons of milk onto the deck. I take my son's name and we crawl toward the massive animal and like babes at their mother's breast, or men at whores' sucked-out titties, we receive the fluids from the old god's chest. I am contented and my soul alights and flies down into the seawater like a sea bird chasing its foreseen whitedark disappearing prey.

My wife now carries my corpse back toward the house. The house is one of a hundred such mythical structures inside of the walls of the island's subdivision. The streets direct us to our dwelling and each one measures the correct quantity of feet-wide and white-lined and yellow dashes and the proper manner to turn left (turning lanes) accompanied by lampposts and traffic signals at regulated intervals. Here the laws and lawns are ideally established, and the manicured green plots line up perfectly in front of every abode and are of the same species of fescue grasses that were first imported from the African savanna by Australian traders one hundred and fifty years ago. The houses are like barricades although they do not protect against the barbarians as the old towers once did, rather it is their duty to decrease the circulation of sight, which they accomplish mightily (just as it is the duty of the roadways to decrease the expanse of the imagination over the land on unformed and as yet untrod footpaths.) The houses, walls, streets, bright lamps and even the nonnative sedge accomplish their considerable task with relative ease, which is, in reality, to screen from visitors and residents alike the nature of the island, just as pornography will distort for the viewer the true breadth and ecstasy of eros.

She brings me back here to my home, and now that I have died I am able to see things as they are: the roles and set pieces of the theatre I inhabited on the island during my lifetime. I can see the sham of it, its shabbiness, the empty comical gestures of my wife and children and all of my neighbors. Only the sunlight and warm archipelago air and moonlight and new green growth on vines and trees and the surf and sea birds remained unadulterated despite the developments contrary to their nature.

And when the monsoon came; and when the waters rose higher than my two story house; and when the winds tore the roofs off of the houses and blew the tarmac out into the sea; and the sky came down in a tidal wave as the wind opened its mouth and held up its fangs to bite off the houses at their cores; the sea waters rising further; and the trees leaning down like giants with giant fingers to break, to cut open—then it was that I understood not only how the weather would eventually remove the glossy sham and silly painted lines and rules and tightly corseted ladies with their ideas of what-to-wears and how-to-looks and how-the-children-should-behaves, but more than this: that it would release us, as it did my rotting corpse, back into a watery grave. That the island would eventually throw off its inhabitants and even its land mass and return like a child to the bosom of the mother, to the sea and the sea floor.

# THE MODERN TIRESIAS

[For the dreamer who arrives tonight to A31 with the glyph of the woman-tree.]

SHE STANDS INSIDE OF HER childhood home once more; it was her grandparents' house and sold off over a decade ago. She sees some of their outdated furniture and objets d'art as if remembering a vivid scene from a novel or film. A red divan, a bronze hanging lamp with inlayed multi-colored glass purchased in the East, a long hallway lined with wooden-framed photographs (of her father her mother her cousins and aunts and of herself as a young girl), two paintings: one of a blue temple and the other a blue mosque, a bronze statuette of a brown bear. She sees behind the furniture and things into the past.

Then she looks down and sees her sex, for she has, unbeknownst to her, removed her clothes. She sees her black pubic hair and toward the top of it, just above the folds of her outer labia, a small penis in a skin sheath, very much like her clitoris, only larger. She begins to play with her new penis; the head is shiny and red like a bright waxed supermarket apple, and by her manipulations it becomes even larger. She thinks how entertaining it is, how she enjoys playing with it: moving the loose skin up and down the new glans, how she might come at any moment. And she begins to think how she understands now what it is to be a man, how much the cock needs the cunt, for she wants only to stick her cock into girls at any cost. Then she wishes she could push this new penis downward at an angle and fuck herself inside of her ancestral home.

# THE PAST

[This dream waited for the dreamer for many years in R97 with the glyph of the half-albatross, half-woman.]

THE BLACK ROAD STRETCHED OUT ahead of him. He walked on the tarmac on the covered earth and he wore no shoes or hat, just worn cotton trousers and a shirt (from another era), and in the offing the sky and land met blue-white (the clouds hung low in the sky like unheavy white stones) to black in an uneven line as if they had been sewn together by an ill-trained or indolent tailor of the same era as the frayed clothes.

He was alone and the landscape was barren of trees but it was obvious to him that at one time there had lived many trees in this earth and not because he could see the stumps of trees, for there were none, but because he felt the keen absence of the winds' arches and resting places; the unecho of birdsongs and untrippings nottrillings from branch to peak; the insects unloudly unsuspended in mid-air triumph of leaves and trunk and vine. He was able to see the notseeable on the road by means of the shivers up his spine and the hackles raised on the back of his neck. And in this manner, he could see animals and plants and men; he could see grief and it was like the seam of the horizon, badly sewn, thick blue white black and scarred upon his cornea. The sun beat down upon the nape of his neck; he sweated; he felt ill. He wanted to vomit onto the tarmac and looked upon the black earth before him and the blue-white powdery sky above. Then the earth changed to resemble a black-and-white photograph, the kind that men used to make when they printed chemical images on paper, so that he saw a silver gelatin land and sky carved among shadows, in greys and blacks; only the whites of men's eyes remained in high contrast. He continued walking and the tarmac did not burn his feet, for he was used to such things as the perpetual absence of shoes, and so the soles of his feet had long ago hardened and cracked and dulled from exposure and use.

A car drives past him and then there are thousands of cars moving alongside him and the cars move without drivers, for he remains the only man; they rush headlong toward the grey horizon and back toward some origin which he cannot see behind him because here in this place there is no beginning, only the tattered seam in front of him, only the forward motions as he progresses, a pilgrim on an undirted road, toward an end which is also unreachable although he has been walking since early in the century, perhaps earlier even than that, since the beginnings of this new era. He is a city man without shoes or hat. He breathes deeply and the car exhaust is bitter in his mouth and nostrils; the black soot collects beneath his nails and inside his nose and mouth as dew once did on the leaves of trees. He cannot stop his forward movement; it is as if he were a dynamo, mechanical, electrical; there is only motion. He is not sure why. He marches toward the black and grey skyline, toward an eschatology that awaits him there. He believes that he will reach his destination and he will become rich and happy and live by the sea in a clean, tight metal fortress. What is the sea? He has by now forgotten about blue and water. The evergreen trees have also faded from his imagination. He forgets the tactile except for the tarmac slapping his feet or his feet, rather, which push against the rocks and formed tar. He has forgotten about his groin. He forgot, many years ago, about books and his family. He forgets about skin, loses his skin now on the pilgrimage. His organs shine outward to the black sky, but he cannot see it or tell of it for his voice has dissipated, the vision snatched back inside the well of his white black eyes. He smells the burning tarmac; it melts beneath his feet and soon each step that he takes takes him farther down into tar and rocks, as if he were walking through black, thick, and burningcold snow. He continues the journey; he is determined. He will arrive at the apogee one day; he knows it; he can smell it, for he has, mysteriously, retained his sense of smell. He smells his stink; he smells the car exhaust (the cars have also vanished from the scene, but they too persist in their absence). He is the blind, mute walker. He heads toward his destiny with a grand gesture. What awaits him there? If the man were not blind, he would be able to see two things: his liver protruding from his spine like a hunk of grey-brown cheese, and in the distance, a towering gale. It runs down the road as if a naked Fury; it is possessed and writhes. Perhaps it is his mother? He had a mother once, and he was once the young, proud, triumphant son.

## THE VISIBLE HIDDEN AWAY GODS I

> *Before such an all-embracing power could establish*
> *itself, a coup d'état had to take place, a long and*
> *extremely slow coup d'état by which the brain's ana-*
> *logical pole was gradually supplanted by the digital*
> *pole, the pole of substitution, of exchange, of conven-*
> *tion, on which are based both language itself and*
> *the vast network of procedures in which we now live.*
> —Roberto Calasso, *Literature and the Gods*

[This one dreamed millennia ago and awaits the new dreamers as Fortune awaits his man.]

THE FIRE ARRIVES INSIDE OF the projectile in time. It cannot evade its trajectory (as the earth [and moon] cannot circumvent its orbit) and decay. The armament arrives from the enemy land (one state, city, garrison, neighborhood over) and like a sea monster released from its chamber of neglected myth, flies now, unstoppably, toward her city. She wonders: is it because men are implacable makers? They cannot forestall the conceiving and making of things? Made houses, made theorems, made guns. Made tensions like thick steel wires.

Made battlefields, Newtonian mechanics, electron microscopes, and interstellar probes. Made the provocation that launched the projectile which now flies through space (and inside the girl's mind, for only the girl knows it was released into air).

The girl waits in her city with her family, her neighbors, and strangers. They eat as they wait; they watch television; they attend religious ceremonies and sit inside dark concert halls; they go to school, to work. They wait for many years, go shopping for years, purchase shoes bags shirts small electronic devices bronze statuettes cars and plastic tubs. They buy and buy (as if to stop it by buying), for although they don't know that it comes, they do sense something is amiss. Meanwhile, it moves unperturbed, unacknowledged (except by the girl) across history and the latest fashion, new news stories and the old galaxy.

The girl is in her beautiful home on the hill. She is a notdreamer. She knows she cannot evade the firestorm or her own demise: it arrives realer than streets and buildings and shops which open and close on time; than new housing subdivisions, sports teams, political parties, and shows; than the modern nations and good jobs, good neighborhoods, good schools; than the laws of the republic; loud speeches from the pulpit, the podium. Than multinational corporations, street gangs, transnational drug cartels, CEOs, CFOs, MGRs, TEMPs, and car salesmen. Than the exchange of goods; codices of the bought and sold. Than the built world.

She tells her family of its pending arrival but they do not listen. They mock her predictions and what they call her demonic vision.

She says: What we hold outside of love, we damn.

Her family begins to fear her. They believe she poses a threat to their line. They decide, after some consideration, to lock the girl inside the dark basement of the beautiful, clean house on the hill. They say she must be kept quiet; she must be contained; it is for her own good.

They descend into the basement in the evening to beat her with blunt sticks and steel wires; they say she does not follow orders; they tell her she must shut it.

She says: The trade winds will not blow.

The sea currents unravel. The gyre widens farther to enclose the ocean and all historical things:

highways, business ventures, sales records

billboards, contracts, medical files

airport runways, intersecting wireways, ships, and international shipping lanes

tall lighted buildings, stout stone fences, antidepressants, anti-narcotics, opioids

cotton sheets, towels, and rags

concertina wire, plastic bags, and a thousand red plastic stirrers;

flat-screen televisions (remotely controlled), laptops, desktops, keyboards,

and magazines stories;

actors on TV like marionettes, like prime ministers, with their bright white-capped teeth speaking hellos;

mobile telephones, artificial sweeteners, hanging clocks,

and the algorithms instrumenting new

mobile telephones, electronic cars, wired houses, and jobs;

applications for jobs, for universities;

universities.

She says: Particulates have filled up the air.

Football-field-sized factories as far as the eye can see. Open pit mines, mountaintop removal mines, strip mines like wounds and new cicatrices. Garbage heaps the size of mountains with the ever-changing pantheons of toasters from Taiwan; tee shirts from San Salvador; school buses from Fort Valley, Georgia; coltan ore from the Democratic Republic of the Congo; and small bits of mica (to make the paint shimmer on the Pacific Coast Highway in the sunlight of Los Angeles on the new sports cars) dug out in Jharkhand.

And because the family cannot keep the girl quiet (somehow she has managed to remove the gag they taped and wired to her skull), and because she will not cease with her ravings—Stop your foolishness, they tell her, or suffer the—they pull the girl's head back by her one thick dark-red plait and while one family member exposes her gullet to the dark basement air and holds her still, another pulls the knife along the skin of her throat to make a new mouth by which the girl, they joke, might further speak her vision.

*She awoke in the myriad nighttime; it was black and she saw with noteyes the apparitions gathered about her bed in H15. I'm hot, they were trying to strangle, I am terrif—. They gathered stronger around her, circled her, cinched her bed, throat, lungs.*

## INSIDE THE POET'S ROOM: DIALOGUE

*Vocatus atque non vocatus Deus aderit.*
—Erasmus, *Adagia*, attributed to the Delphic oracle

— ON THE SEMI-ARID PLAINS, in the high desert, on the distant atoll of the archipelago, in the cold forests of the north

—

— inside of the weather

—

—recall the young man in the old tragedy, how he understood this knowledge

—

—too late;

—

— in the unlanguage spaces

—

—recall where gods once resided.

—Had they departed?

—A necessity thereby caused his mother to consume son's flesh (it was the god's induced madness made her do it, the old story goes): she chewed the meat from the young king's shinbones

— He cried out, *Mother*?

—after she first hunted him in the wood, tracking the buck (she saw only animal when she snared him).

—

—The son as sacrifice,

—

—the house.

—And afterwards, when she realized what she'd done?

—

*WHAT DO YOU KNOW? YOU who believe what you can see. Can you see the trees that stood on the rise one hundred fifty years ago? The sky uncity-electrified and gloriously starry in the black night? Can you see the virus that only a moment ago touched onto your finger into your eye and now runs through your body in the blood as if on a concourse? How your cells march and fall asunder like men fighting on the streets?*

*Can you see me?*

*Do not forget the third rule of the house: that each visitor is permitted only the one night. I am not just your caretaker*, she says.

※

THIRTEEN WHITE-FRAMED WINDOWS FACE ONTO the moor. The backside of the house is red-brick and blind. The windows look out like eyes and appeal to the traveler to come here. Here the dream for the aspiring politician, for the university graduate with his diploma and no understanding. The headmaster without pupils, the headmistress with her thick primer of rules. The hunter who lives in a desert metropolis, quiescent and idle, he hunts for television programs, fights alongside actors and athletes of dramas and football games. For the middle and upper classes midway through their lives and out of place, taking each corner of land for its houses, each corner of air for its breath, each pipe for its water, each water for its thirst, each cereal for its, animal for its, meals. The suicide in the rich girl, the suicide in the poor. For the boy who lived in a house when he was young, his favorite house he said, and behind the house a wood ("they were my woods") who now lives in the cold grey city and holds the memory of the wood as he does of the old man (a ghost) who bade him goodnight at bedtime each evening. It was not real, he thinks; it was only my imagination: the enchanted place, the spirit. (My job is real, my bank accounts, disappointments, family history, and future goals.)

The house is two stories with four long interior hallways painted the dim brown-green of a faded vine. At the end of the hallway with the seven doors to the seven rooms where the travelers sleep, an illuminated light in the shape of a small half-globe attaches to the wall above one of the house's thirteen eyes. The glass of the window's four panes scarcely increases the light inside the building, any more than the dim electrical source secured above it. Midway down the corridor, a newly painted steel radiator heats the space during the cold, wet winters; a large fire extinguisher encased in a glass box hangs above it in a comical nod to the outside, transitory requirements and building codes of the state. Four metal pipes run the length of the hallway's ceiling and they add to the effect of standing inside a long tunnel. The light at the end does not mark the terminus or draw the travelers toward it but instead accentuates the length and darkness of the old green corridor and the strangeness of the seven rooms which pull off from it like roots pushing down from the base of a tree trunk into the darker, distant soil of the underworld.

# TWO

# THE FUTURE

THE MAN AWAKENS ALONE FOR his beloved has left him. He feels cold inside of the brick house and he knows that in twenty years' time he will die in a hospital bed with over-washed white synthetic bedding and machine wires running up his arms, the nurses outside in the hallway who ignore and don't admire him, the doctor who missed all his calls, and no children, no familiar smells or familiar lifefullness inside of the modern edifice. No one to touch his hand, his cheek; cradle the old man's body, thin arms, thin legs, and pot-belly. No one to sing to him or say his name with love. He is afraid and he clings to notdying. He doesn't follow the edges of his breath or the heart that beats in his chest in a bloody solitude.

On a metal skiff now on the seas in the north. Everything will become the dark blue-grey of winter soon and he sees the tall, magnificent mountains sidle away from his gaze down the long corridor of the waterway as if to infinity, as if he were seeing them inside a house of mirrors and not from the bow of this small skiff. He feels their immense power when he looks down at the mountains in the grey water reflections and up at the endless range.

On the northern seas, the bull whale sings. For whom or to what does the animal do it? To its mate? To the ocean and its vast caves?

Then the man is on an island far out in the Pacific and he is reunited with the beloved. She is kind; she opens her legs lovingly; she is naked and unhateful of the nakedness of his portly, unsunned, wrinkled flesh; his skinny legs and veiny, bruised arms; his overfed, diseased body and its open sores and dry skin. He puts his penis into the young girl; he puts his small penis into the universe and returned.

# THE FULL MOON

I STAND IN FRONT OF my home with my neighbors in the city of B. The air is red-tinted and I look up into the nightred sky and see the full moon; the full moon looks down at me with its white eye. There is no break to the looking and the looker so that the moon is looking up at the moon and I look down at me and we are traveling out beyond the seeing and death is looking and no-I is looking and happiness is there in the merger so that the cosmic loneliness ends and the looker-looked and seer-seen and light-lighted and we have spread out like a black galaxy bird in flight so that the heart which feeds the blood, the lungs which oxygenate un—          I break the moon's hold (or the moon breaks from me, eye from eye). I am afraid to travel farther and I look again to my neighbors, continue the story of my day, of loves denied, of the drama of lost employment, of the highest-felt feelings of new purchases, new resentments, remembered slights, plumbing problems, recipes for chicken on the bone. (The black white-light galaxy behind the red sky, the full white moon, still calling continuously.)

The moon awakens me later that night at two a.m. and for no reason I can ascertain it is always 2 a.m. when the moon pushes through the window and stares down into the sleeping girl and awakens the dreamer and it is anxiety? The moon makes a call once the sleeper has descended, but its old language is difficult to decipher: what does it mean? And is it the light that makes the call? Or is it the gravitational pull of the satellite at perigee (and how the earth, like a cunt, like the girl, takes the full moon's forces unto itself)?

The moon awakens me again tomorrow and I am again willfully dumb. The notdreamer stares at the white orb. The moon is realest so might I one day recognize itselfness?

# THE END OF THE LOVE AFFAIR I

THE GIRL AND THE BOY are traversing icy terrain. She doesn't feel the inclement weather although she wears only lightweight city clothing: cotton pants and a short-sleeved tee shirt. She has old tennis shoes on her feet. They are atop a glacier inside of a beautiful bay and he tells her how they will walk down the precipice and she tells him that she can't do it, that she wears the wrong shoes and she will slip on the steep icy mountain and break her spine in two. She will suffer. He says not to worry, that he will guide her, she will be fine, and he moves closer to her to take her hand; the sky is a grey, flat board above her head and his; the white-blue ice descends before them widely. She has a feeling of vertigo; she has a feeling that the glacier has a will and that this will will pull her down its surface. Her breath is marked and heavy and all around the white-blueness is in front of her eyes. Strangely, she does not feel cold.

Then there is no longer ice; there is only blue everywhere: the sky opens up like a river into the brightest cerulean she can ever recall seeing; she looks down and the glacier has metamorphosed and gem-like blue waters rush forth below.

Then there is no water. Now there are thousands of humans (like ants she thinks, vermin) running across the new sludge of the moor, enormously deep human footprints have turned the earth into a brown mud quilt of footprints and crushed grasses and black wet earth and destruction everywhere. As far as the beloved can see, there is electric human natural chaos, for only man exists now, only his rages, desires, ideas, and unmet passions. The beloved sees brown mud, brown water; she does see not see radical blue or ice whites any longer anywhere.

Then she has returned to the suburb she lived in as a child. She is now a teacher of native dance and she instructs her students to stretch their bodies and become lithe and stronger and in this way, more attractive. A celebrated blonde actress attends her class at the dance studio and the girl feels happy that a famous and beautiful woman, like a new queen, is following her imprecise, ill-informed dance instructions (for in actuality, she knows very little about the subject she teaches). When the class ends, the blonde accompanies the girl to her home and stays a short while. The blonde deposits a note wrapped around a small bundle of tax receipts onto the dining room table when she leaves. The note and its secret message is written in the antiquated and dead Urartian tongue and for this reason it is indecipherable to the neophyte.

# THE NEITHER I, NOR YOU, HE SHE

*For seeing things as separate is the sole cause of otherness.*
—Adi Shankara

HE IS NOT HE SHE not she, a notI dreams the she he I, or dreams you wildly as if the wind winded itself across the moors, or the waves waved one hundred yards in the distance, or the wings winged, and the sun sunned its selves: trees treeing and the fires unstoppable fireness. I dream a she and she walks in the nighttime grey matter of dreams which appear, as always, as notdreams. She is on an aeroplane and she is talking to the passengers next to her. The aeroplane is like an autobus and soon the pilot walks to the back of the vehicle and opens a bottle of red wine and although he doesn't offer her any libations, the passengers at her right and left drink greedily from their filled glasses.

The plane has now landed and she is surprised because she could not feel its descent and her ears did not pop and her sinus membranes did not explode silently and horrifically as they often do when the plane comes down from the middle of the sky. Then they are driving on the highway inside of the aeroplane (as if on an autobus) and the pilot stops miles from the airport near the center of the city; from here we must walk to the airport, the pilot announces. The passengers disembark from the machine. Now I am waiting at a street corner for the light to change. Where are my things? Did I pack a bathing suit for my vacation on the island? Is my lover meeting me and how will he reach me if I do not possess a telephone or know where I am where is the city of—?

She crosses the street inside of two white painted lines when the traffic light changes to green. She moves with the hundreds of passengers and residents in the tarmac city past the concrete steel buildings, the steel and aluminum vehicles, advertisements on signboards. The people move together like an animal herd; the herd runs inside two white painted lines toward the cement barriers, high-rises. I move and she moves, all of the people move through the city. I and she and he and you are moved along; the wind the wave the sunlight the sea, we all move together.

## THE PUZZLE

HE AWAKENS IN THE MIDDLE of the night and he has found the solution. He will try and recall it for morning. Sleeps again; falls in. The problem is the labyrinth and he is inside it when he thinks that he is out; the in and out unfollowing in and out regulations so that in is not inner, and out is never available, or the feeling of out is like awakening from a dream which is another dream inside a box of the dream, and dreams inside of dream boxes, larger inside of smaller, like nesting dolls which do not follow the laws of classical mechanics and are synchronic mythical structures about which he briefly understood something, as if finding a solution to a problem, and then he slept again and forgot it by morning.

SHE GOES TO THE BRICK house of a notvolition which is the volition of the dead who await her, who cannot attend her any longer in the city (in that overly noisy, busy world): they lie in wait like the tides lie in wait for her here. The white beacon on the promontory does not warn with its whiteness of impending danger but rather signals her to this territory, into the cavern of the house, down the corridor with its seven lettered and numbered iconic doors, to enter inside of the room, the womblike structure, alone and matronly calling, called her: she is rung up and told that she can arrive in one week's time (it is an invitation, but as with some gifts, ought not be refused).

The dead await behind the rosewood doors. Listen, they say.

# THREE

## NEW LOVE I

SHE HAS SEEN THE LOVER two times and on their second outing he kissed behind her ear on the back of her neck. And how did he know when he doesn't yet know the beloved, or she herself understand her desires (or how it is when the girl is on the cusp of new love, which is very much like the quiet places at the back of the sea before the swift current moves in) that this spot on her neck arouses her most of all? Today he begins to move down her spine. He lifts her onto his back and he carries her as he would carry his own mother. He bears her down the path and they begin to cross the river. They circle and entwine; he moves his arm over her arm, and his heart or thighs or cock vibrate, push against her body, lean into, move down her spinal cord into her labia, her thighs, her feet. This is a beginning? she thinks, and she begins to feel afraid, for there is always unaccountable dread at the threshold. It climbs up into her visions and the old father, the old lovers, return. They beat her, berate her, tell her that it is all for naught. And then the old husband arrives; he has walked through the mud and stands at the embankment; he shakes his tired black fist toward her from a distance: *Bitch*, he says, *not for you; you open your legs too callously, dirty.*

But she will look at you and say something trivial about an incident at a roadside restaurant and you will laugh and lift her higher

49

onto your back as you reach the other side of the river. And there inside of your laugh-tones the girl falls down and lies like a child on the early summer grasses beneath the impending light of the crepuscule as it slips down softly and orange red-yellow to cover her body and the earth.

# TWO MOONS

SHE ACCOMPANIES TWO STRANGE WOMEN, one of whom she trusts although she cannot say wherefore. They are walking on an open plain and stumble upon an old man seated on a metal folding chair. He is alone; he points his index finger skyward. The girl looks up and makes a loud, hitched scraping sound as she inhales, for in the sky above her an enormous waxing gibbous moon both yellow and fat is rising, and a short distance from it, hanging wildly, another gibbous moon (or perhaps it is a planet, she thinks), reddish and fat and beautiful, waxes in the opposite direction of the yellow, as if it were in the southern hemisphere, or she were in both hemispheres simultaneously. And the girl feels awe for the beauty she perceives and terror for the disorder and disharmony of two moons where there ought only be one. Am I dying? Are these the natural wars?

She thinks about brown bears, the old salmon, and the great blue whales: their manner of electrifying the air, the water (before the invention of rifles and stiff-jack armaments and radar, and even afterwards). When she sees them on the mountain path and they cross beneath the hull of her guide's small boat, tipping it thereby, then she can remember—here, look—then she knows: see the black brown bear scat on the old spoor; the muscular run of the cohos in early fall; the humpback that now breaches in front of the small skiff: *you are small*. And the knowledge opens out from her like a revelation, whirls up toward the two waxing gibbous moons and back down to the strange girl on whom this girl feels that she can inexplicably rely.

She takes the hand of the girl, a demigod, and she offers herself. First love then death, the demigod says, and the three leave the old man behind and continue their journey on the open plain beneath the yellow and red moons' light toward the high mountain which waits, like an idol, in the distance and calls to them to ascend.

# THE END OF THE MARRIAGE

THERE IS A WOUND THAT runs along the stomach, the vagus nerve, through the four chambers of the heart, and higher still toward the base of her throat so that it hurts in this region of her body. It is a notphysical injury to her selfness, her ideas of the future, of the family, which she had once given her cells and tissues over to.

Therefore, she drives her car to her husband's new house. In front of his driveway, the blue four-door sedan of the newgirl is parked. This is the girl to replace her. And he has taken the dog, and he has taken the dish, and he has taken her boys to this new place. He fucks the newgirl now; he is putting his cock into the unwifely cunt, licking the cunt hairs with his cuckolded tongue. And the adulteress' children sleep, dream; tomorrow, they think, we will have a chocolate and cold milk.

As the marriage ends, the wife walks down the street of her mind and knocks on the doors of her sundry manly desires. See the man at Door 1: he is kind and bold and rich and his toes bend backwards like squid cooked in their ink. Door 2 is well dressed and fat and happiest when his tongue laps gently at her vaginal mouth. Door 3 sweats profusely (see his stained tee shirts in a large pile behind him), while Door 4 collects art and writes modern tragedy for the theatre. There is a fifth door and another. The doors are without numbers, in actuality, but she has numbered them here for the sake of order. Each door leads into a room and at the back of that room there is another door: all the inside doors lead to one central chamber. Inside of this room there stands a throne and upon it sits a man, the king, the father on his old beaten metal folding chair in the middle of the heptagon. *Welcome daughter,* he says, *back home.*

# THE ANGELIC

*The map of Babylon shows the city at the center of a
vast circular territory bordered by a river, precisely
as the Sumerians envisioned Paradise. This partici-
pation by urban cultures in an archetypal model is
what gives them their reality.*
—Mircea Eliade, *The Myth of the Eternal Return:
Or, Cosmos and History*

THE ANGELIC LIVES INSIDE A walled city. All of the cities
of her nation like all of the cities of the earth have sealed off their
territories. The barriers are cracked cement bollards in ancient Bagh-
dad and old Mexico City; in the corners of Jerusalem the immense
steel mirrors of the victors (who in recent memory had been the
vanquished) hold the reflections of the local dogs who burrow and
beg beyond the glossy metal frontier. The walls reemerge tall and
spindly like black wire bird cages in Berlin. And in all of the United
States of America the highest quality, the most beautiful technologi-
cally advanced apparatus stretches across mountains, over rivers, and
through the Sonoran Desert like a steel serpent to menace the weary
trespasser with barbed and steel talons. Lagos and Tegucigalpa use

broken glass bottles embedded into the tops of high walls to cut up invaders. New Delhi and Madrid employ clay scissors they sharpened into ferocious, chthonic teeth.

Helicopters fly constantly over my city, the Angelic says, as she winds her fair hair into round questions at the back of her skull.

Inside the walled city, the young seek adoration, amusement, and employment. Boys seek colorful moving pictures of cunts, cocks, and asses; narcotics; and cheap succor; girls do the same. Unmanned planes fly without surcease, so that the skies are loud, machine-filled, replete with white metal wasps and electric flies. The walls wall-in people, but not the noise, so that the mechanical racket carries out to a wall-less horizon few can perceive. Here inside this city, each citizen carries his national identification code embedded into plastic inside the fleshy pad of his thumb ("for ease of recognition and your personal safety"); each constituent pays his groceries, enters exits the bank, checks into and out of airports, arrives to and leaves his workplace, his apartment building, with his thumb pressed onto a small black IDer mounted onto a wall. And an invisible machine reads the individual's invisible number and this number moves through the loud machined sky to arrive at a room where it can be categorized, calculated, recorded, assessed, and controlled by another machine invisible to all but the machine's owner and operators. The unmanned planes and helicopters protect the skies, the banks, the grocery stores, the corporation, the nation from the robbers, the invaders, the ill-suited, the indigent, the foreigner, migrants, the drugged terror outside the perimeters of the cities of America and of Europe, Israel, China, and Japan—and from the terror inside the cities (inside the mind) that encroaches willy-nilly nevertheless.

The Angelic, with tied-up questions (of love) at the back of her head, wonders how she might comprehend a silence twisted into the strands of her light brown hair. She waits patiently for answers. She is unafraid to know them.

# LOVE

BRIGHT ORANGE ROCKWEEDS COVER THE old coastal rocks of the middle intertidal zone as far as the eye can see. Thousands of tiny sea snails make their home among them and a polka-dot pattern with their delicate black shells. On the rocks nearest the water line, the orange-black tapestry curtails and the uncountable (more than millions), silent, immutable acorn barnacles hold fast. They cluster one next to the other in tightly knitted constellatory patterns; in abeyance they do not stand or sit but wait (as the rocks wait) for the tides to come in, for the largest full and new moon spring tides.

The stone animals appear unalive, unmagical in the cold air of the low tide. They are closed and sharp-cutting and she kills them as she walks on top of them. She crushes orange, bulbous seaweed, black periwinkle snails, and then climbing down the massive steely rocks for a closer view of the northern sea, smashes barnacles with her heavy water-proof rubber boots: the world upon world of white-grey carapaces, their cosmos unhinged and destroyed.

But the tide will come in; it does. Now submerged. And the hard animal which seemed not an animal (to her) only moments ago opens itself to the sea. A six-fingered appendage emerges from the shell mouth and waves its long six-pronged catcher out for sustenance (like children waving flags at a parade), pulls back, then moves out again. It and the uncountable others cross the once-dry sealed threshold to grasp something with their white, feathery fingers, fall back, seek once more. This is yearning, she thinks; see them: a legion of gossamer appendages waving from their cone-shaped hearths (like delighted children) to grab their livelihood from the fluids. Repetition is no repetition for the acorn barnacle. And even the smallest, most inconsequential creatures…, she thinks. (Inconsequential to whom?)

She leans down from her perch on the orange rockweed-covered rocks. The killing sounds of periwinkles and plants climb into her ears, the crush and crumble, and she sees in the rising seawater the graceful sublime beauty of the delicate limbs that emerged from their sharp, hard domes with the new tide and reenter their domains silently (to her deaf ears), exit again, as if unto eternity.

Today she noticed them for the first time when she stopped for a moment and looked down, beheld what she had not before—for before, the white acorn barnacle was merely a calcified nuisance to trample with her feet. It was her guide who showed her the lower intertidal zone, he lifted small stones, turned them over to reveal the world underneath: tiny purple spotted crabs rushed out, and clinging limpets. He said, *See here.*

This is the same man who later will take the girl to his underground cavern and show her her own metamorphosis inside of his lair.

# THE THEATRE IN THE MIND

SHE IS IN A LUSH green garden and two king cobras battle fiercely. They rise up taller and their upper ribs and neck bones flatten wider to make a large canopy of their hoods while they violently do battle and rush across the stage. Now she watches them from a distance behind glass, for she is safe inside of her home and locks the doors and looks down and there is another snake which then becomes a green lizard with the eyes and nose of a child's stuffed animal, the kind that can be purchased from any corner store. She drops the toy onto the floor and opens the refrigerator, but there is no inside of it. Her neighbor enters the kitchen and says it is time for the performance and she won't need any props in her role as LEADING LADY; he will play the LEADING MAN, he says. She is nervous for she doesn't know her lines, and the audience listens attentively. Soon it is her cue to come on stage, which is the garden grasses, and walk alongside the man who is her lover and tell him in her long and strident monologue that she has not died, that together they may lie in the lap of the ancient avatar, the thousand-headed cobra, and look up to see the cosmos resting inside the folds of its many hoods suspended above them like a thousand brightly colored lamps.

The show finishes, the time of make-believe ends. The actors huddle around the notstage (for years) until the director says they will do it again! Play their parts one more time. LEADING LADY looks at the script in her hands and reads her lines as if to memorize them, although she already knows the outcome. They are only performing the third act tonight. LEADING LADY and LEADING MAN sit together cross-legged in the lap of the thousand-headed cobra to ready themselves. She rubs his feet and he puts his hand at the nape of her neck to find the bridge between them.

## NEW LOVE II

SHE MOVES INTO THE CUL-DE-SAC of your voice and lies in-side its perimeter for a moment, as if inside a room, and thinks that here she feels at ease. There are other matters. There are your muscular thighs, your large cock. There is the question she has about the white flecks scattered throughout your blue irises like tiny bits of brilliant mica in sand, how you pulled her hair back stiffly when you wanted to fuck her and she became more aroused. In her moments of nervous distrust, she will listen to you carefully and settle near t and p or lie next to a vowel in your breath's hitches happily—o—and afterwards, m or n. Inside the edifice of your voice, surrounded by its particular timbre, she thinks of a favorite uncle, or her first lover when she was eighteen. She is old now: grey-haired and desirous and she has loved and abandoned and fucked many men. You are old also and your feet have widened and broken with age. She called you on the telephone this evening for the tones she seeks: the mystery of their consolation and the structures they make in her mind. You are speaking and she is speaking and not words or meaning, nothing but o moves into the ear's blind channel and marks the beginning of a love affair as light-ning on the edge of the horizon indicates the heating up and expan-sion of the air, portends the sound of thunder and the rain which thereupon falls down.

THIRTEEN EYE-WINDOWS STARE DOWN ONTO the moor but the land does not return the slow stolid look of the house.

Inside the corners of the brick building, in the closets and enclosed spaces, the old, the residual, the neglected, the forlorn, and other potencies lurk and abide. They emerge at night when they can more easily see the traveler. They give him his dream; they give the girl in the next room hers. They have guarded the dread of the ocean and tall mountains and tall bridges; the hurt children, hurt animals (slaughtered without ritual); demigods who refused to leave; the coastal rocks; the cave dwellers of anxiety; rejected lovers; the swollen genitalia; moons; air; daemons and tricksters; ravaged plants and minerals; the looming planets; the stars', the nebulae's, the galaxies' roar; the primeval forest. Why have they all gathered here? Was the brick house made to house them, or did they find the brick house and settle inside it, as if into an embrace? A nexus of land, sky, wind, and sea.

The house retains its forces, but it does not keep the travelers for more than one night. In the morning, he awakens, he rises and attends his ablutions, drinks a glass of water, and eats a small breakfast placed onto a tray and left in front of his door. There is fruit; there is bread and butter and jams. He descends to the first floor and the caretaker escorts him to her vehicle. She drives him back to the ferry building (they are both silent the while) where he purchases a ticket to return with his black valise to his southern city on the coast. One can say that a change has occurred, one can say, even, that the dream resides in a new form: it does not end when he departs; on the contrary, it continues inside of the building. *Goodbye*, the caretaker says, surprising him with the sound of her voice when he opens the door to step down from the vehicle. *Remember to remember in your dreamcity.*

When one speaks of the brick house, one must also speak of the light that does not shine. The electric lights are lighted but they do not illuminate the darkness: the foul green paint extinguishes the light; the closets extinguish the light; the despair and loneliness, the closed heart of the traveler who visits with his sombering fear.

It is winter when he arrives and it is always the time when the sun has just set. The sky is blue-blackening and has become the same dark color as the tarmac road that passes the brick house and winds down the incline toward the old lighthouse and the sea.

And the questions move across his mind like water over stones: how does the old and indifferent caretaker subsist outside of the economies? Why is she no kinder upon my departure, no more interpretable about the edges of her skin or blood? What are her duties at the brick house? (Who is her employer?) Who prepared the breakfast that arrived at my door on a tray at 6:15 a.m.? (Why this hour?) How is it that I awakened so early (unusual for me for I have always been a man who sleeps late; I awaken only with the aid of an alarm clock and begrudgingly)? And how is it that I never for a moment considered breaking any of the house rules (when normally I seek to contravene)? And who repairs and repaints (the inclement weather of the moor) the white windows and eaves and maintains the shorn grasses and keeps everything clean and orderly looking? Who owns this property (for ours is a nation of private ownership of every thing)? Whose money, which funds, deposited into which bank accounts, support the enterprise? And how is it that the only payment asked of me was the night inside N49? He ponders these questions (and not others he does not or cannot articulate but which, nevertheless, swirl in the eddies of his mind.) He decides that he knows only this: the house called and he arrived.

# FOUR

# ALTITUDE

THEY WALK ON A DIRT path along the steep edge of a mountain. She walks next to a man in his fifties who is shorter than her and dark haired and a gypsy, someone yells out from behind, from southern Spain. She is a bourgeois and for that reason she wears expensive new clothes including a short, tight shirt that reveals her abdomen (in keeping with the fashion of the season). Later he will press his hand to her bellyskin and she will think how she wants to become his lover even though he is old and foreign and the teeth in the front of his mouth are no longer white but yellowed and rimmed in the brown becoming black of decay (and his fat belly, his sour breath, scarred skin, tattered and dirty clothes.) She wants him to desire her foremost.

An entourage of friends walk behind them, for they have all come out for this excursion into the mountains and encountered the gypsy by chance in the wilderness. They walk closer to the clouds and blue sky, and all around are sharp peaks and this could be the Sierra Nevada, the tallest granite mountains in the contiguous United States. The dark-haired man says he is from an old culture as he guides her across the vast landscape.

She notices a pack of raucous boys on the adjacent mountain chain. They are separated from her group by a large chasm but they are easy to see nonetheless. The half-dozen boys skate along the rims of the sharp peaks: they stand at a summit on the thinnest edge of rock and dirt and rush down it and then up the next, down and up and down again, as if they were riding a rollercoaster at an amusement park. The wild group of boys skim the razors' edges while she watches them, as if the mountains were not mountains but lines and curves in the shape of black letters. They ride down the diagonal of M and then up the round part of a U and down and up another U, and on the other side of the black lines the white spaces wait, so that the girl is scared for the boys' safety. The gypsy is unperturbed as he watches the incautious, unrestrained boys. He presses his hand against her bellyskin and she inexplicably wants this strange and foreign and ugly small man to take her away from this excursion with friends and the charred meats they burnt earlier on an outdoor grill, and the empty conversations, the hahahas, the we-eat, we-win, we-are-beautiful, young, and improved.

The boys continue to rush down and up the contours of the old Roman letters near the clouds while death trails them with joy. The calm old gypsy with the black-rimmed teeth, sour breath, ragged clothes; the city people terrified of mountains, of thin air, the abyss, and of these unafraid, mad boys.

From there, the gypsy leads the girl to a cave. And from inside the cavern the dead arise and call out their unheeded, unreasonable, ancient lore—unmodern, untimely, bloody, and—which, like the voices of the old beings and nonbeings, throng and merge and possess all who enter here.

# GALATEA

THE INVENTOR PUTS HIS THOUGHTS into the machine, the girl he makes. She is tall or short and blonde or brunette, fat or skinny (he does, however, insist on medium-large to very large tits). He constructs the manikin: she is kind and intelligent and passionate (licks his balls and anus happily). She prepares delicious meals, bears his children, keeps his house and accounts, looks at him lovingly, like this:

He intertwines the girl's cells with his, like a woman sews thread through cloth. It is a vibration he makes; it is like love; love is like this: the chemical bonding whereby attraction overcomes repulsion. Her cells are electrical sockets and he is the singular plug.

Now that he's made her, he waits for her to arrive. Instead of attending his fate at home, however, he boards an aeroplane and travels to a foreign city where he doesn't speak the language. He lives in a motel in a run-down suburb on the outskirts of the city for many months. He works at his computer and he awaits a sign. He watches TV when he is not working. In late spring, he drives to a stranger's house in the city center for a business dinner and she opens the front door of the house when he rings the bell. She is the stranger's wife and she escorts him to the dining room for their meal. His own blindness makes her unseeable at first (like the bonded atoms inside his palms) until the current begins the pull of he-to-she and she-to-he and four weeks later he meets her for a secret rendezvous and puts his penis inside of the girl's body, like an offering or a closed circuit (for without this closure, electricity cannot be transformed), and then he knows what his memory unremembered and his recognition at first notknew until her cunt confirms for him that she is, in fact, the girl he made.

And although he and his beloved do not speak the same language, and although her tits are smaller than average, they return together to his country of origin and his ardor is in no way deleteriously affected.

# THE UNDERGROUND BATHHOUSE

EVERYTHING IS SHADES OF GREEN, chartreuse to dark pine, among the small and large plants in the primeval wood. Invisible birds sing invisible birdsongs. The small nuisance of biting insects attacks her exposed skin. He holds the girl's red-polished, clean-nailed hands (his brown dirt fingernails, his wide-spread, unshod feet), *Come along*, he says, and she looks at his legs and sees they have become the legs of a buck. He prances in front of her, his human-muscled torso, brown beard on his face, and eyes which bluely smile as if into the edifice of her heart. He laughs and the sound moves around the treed lands and like steam rises to the canopy overhead and beyond, into the sky, and then back down and down her spine to rest at its base like a coiled snake. *Take my hand*, he says. She has alighted onto his back and he runs them to the cedar-wood cavern and opens the door. He steps down the dark, hot sweet cedar-smelling stairs; she holds his back and she is electrified and aroused, and he then is the man again and guides her to lie supine on a wooden pallet. The steam rises in the dark heat of the bathhouse. She is unclothed and looks at her naked body and sees that here in the underground cavern her hair has grown unaccountably, reaches to her knees, and her arms are unmarked by age or sun or insect bites, and her feet do not ache any longer or the herniated disc in her back. He says, *Turn over*, and he begins to wash her, pushes a sponge down her thighs, around her calves, along the feet, and up to her shoulders, beneath her arms, her neck; the water is warm and soothing and the soap smells of lemon and sage. He has language but he no longer uses it; she has lost speech to the heat and vortex down where he spins them. She cannot see clearly in the cavern, but she senses that his cock is engorged as he rubs her with his big hands on the inside of her thighs as she imagines he would touch the inside folds of her cunt if they were fucking. He lifts her by her arms and she tucks her chin to her chest and her hair falls up out of the cavern and into the woods and he begins to wash her hair slowly, first with the hot water, she tilts her head back, then cold, and removes the lesions of grief, machine noise, parking lots, business hours, meeting times, car accidents, traffic jams, and the dollars she makes and spends carelessly, the TV shows she consumes (like a drug) after work each night. He takes all of her efforts—to buy, to advance in her career, to own, to worry, to slink down greed's rough road, to eat factory foods and factory meats—and puts it down the length of her hair. And the hair flows back into the dirt, into the fire, and her labia softens, reddens, opens further; her clitoris becomes stiff and engorged; she is cunt-wet and her secretions drip from her thighs onto the pallet and she recovers words; she calls out for him to attend her, for his fingers, his tongue, cock, and horns. And her hair now falls off like the lizard's tail and becomes dirt again. *Fuck me*, she says. He will not. He bathes her, remakes as reminds in the cavern the latent, the indwelling feelings in her. And she is sweating and she is thirsty, and like a newborn, hairless, and then she is asleep and dreams. She dreams in circles. Of hallways and walls and factories and dirty hospital rooms. Of old abandoned houses filled with malicious spirits, and loud elevators that ascend and creak loudly; of a dark basement in a house on a hill; of the heptagon at the center of her thoughts. She awakens as the demigod lovingly opens her chest with his horns and removes the red meat from her body in payment for the bath; she watches her blood soak into his beard as he eats her heart muscle. And she dips her fingers into her open chest cavity and extends her red-nailed, red-bloodied hand toward him as greater offering for this new clean body he has given her today.

# THE GYRE

> DIONYSUS: *You do not know the limits of your strength. You do not know what you do. You do not know who you are.*
>
> — Euripides, *Bacchae*

THE WATER IS BLACK AND the sun's light black-green. You stand alone at the ship's bow (the other passengers huddle below deck; it is -30° Fahrenheit outside) and watch how before you the massive icebreaker cuts through the frozen sea. The ice is a long, flat sheet in front of you, and black water wakes behind you, tremendous and loud.

You have left that place and now travel in the country of the subtropical gyre. It is warmer here and here the sea was once filled with floating kelp beds as large as islands which moved untethered from horizon to horizon in green, orange jubilant masses. Now in lieu of the old seaweed archipelagos, a continent's width of plastics tumble and sink: the cities' detritus and your discards from the coffee shop, the hundred red plastic stirrers you used for a moment (day after day as the sun rises) to stir the sugar into your coffee and afterwards deposited into large plastic garbage bags. And then (and then: thousands of coffee shops, restaurants, cities, towns, countries as the sun rises) months and years later it all moved down a river into the sea, to gather here in the middle of the ocean, northeast of the islands in the Pacific: the bottles, red stirrers, yellow, white, and green bags; the cases for soda, computer hulls, trays, and nylon nettings; the tubs and buckets; casings; counters, cups, chairs, beds, and balls; the bottle caps and bottle ties and orange prescription bottles from the pharmacy; medical gloves, medical hoses, medical gowns, and outdated medical equipment; the containers from your lunch, dinner, and afternoon snacks. Here they float and turn down into the depths and on the waves and with the wind, the layers of plastic animals which animals now ingest as you will also along the chain of the eaten, small to large, back into your belly, when you consume, eventually, the red stirrer you tossed yesterday into the coffee shop trash bin. Your children (and theirs) will have it. And on this will go, the gyre widening out until the plastic immortal creatures (like new immortals?) one day reach your shore. They will endure a millennium, a university scientist says (another insists it will be ten thousand, fifty, one hundred thousand years) in the sea. They do not decompose (like your body inside of the brick house: what kinds of newgods are these?); their only change is to become smaller. They are, for us, eternity in the middens.

See all of the factories in all of the cities producing the small, colored plastic pellets of which all other plastic goods eventually will be formed. They are no bigger, these pellets, than the black eye inside the coho salmon's newly laid orange egg. Reds, blues, yellows, greens, oranges, and whites: the colorful pieces travel the earth's surface on the roads and in barges and aeroplanes toward factories in all of the cities (as the sun rises) and are formed into bags, bottles, cups, tools, toy car parts, belts, bands, machine components, automobile parts, player pieces, mops, and brooms. And you know in your dream that this one will outlast many others, will outlive the paper-made books and paper-made monsters. The leviathan himself—silent, white, and immense, long dead now—had his belly filled-to with the monstrous carnival of colorful food-looking objects: a forty-three-foot fishing

74

net, two buckets, one car engine cover, seventy-six shopping bags and a BIC lighter. This is the ten- fifty- one-hundred thousand-year polyethylene myth on the polyethylene earth, of the insides of bones tangled up in polyurethane wrath.

Down you'll go, into the gyre. Spin out into the dream and this dream lies just before the horizon of destruction, in the midst of the worldwide production of things. These are the undying, the unfeeling—they don't conduct heat or even terror like the wolf, the bear who once lived in your wood, the girl whose groin rises the fire in you, the old spirits who live in the creek and tree hollows—which you denied in favor of what you believed you controlled?

Dream of the earth. Dream of dying (which is also to live). Dream of the Sitka spruce, lighter green western hemlocks, of red cedars and a yellow. See the rare yellow wood as it burns. Dream of the forest, of animals with lungs the size of your body, and of the humpback who surfaced just as he and then you breathed in unison. Dream of the air. Dream the mystery of photosynthesis. Dream of trees and of not shaping them into futures, removing them like plastic dolls from plastic shelves. Dream of what is to come. Of laughter on the edges of things. Of holy love in the holy cunt and cock: love in all the forms. Of the interstitial lovers: the girl in the byre and the hunter who came for her. Dream of the hunter who is now armed with rifles, submarines, trapeze bomber planes, money-filled bank accounts, and of how he forgot his name.

Dream of places apart. Of the coastal grasslands and the sedges and rushes where the brown bear rambles, eating them in late summer (the cohos have not yet returned and he is ravenous). Dream of knowledge as you would of candy. Dream of fucking all of the hunters with your maiden fantasy. Dream of books like boats (books like portals): they lift the dreamer out of the gyre. Undream the gyre. Undream the cutted woodlands. Undream steam engines and combustion engines, quarterly profits, and the miracle of petrol. Undream department store chains, fast food chains, the International Monetary Fund, and the factories where men are concentrated like vermin at a fish-and-tackle store. Dream behind the city; dream the rivers behind the unrivered lands; dream on top of mountains, of clouds which sit lazily like girls on their peaks in white-grey formations. And the sea, fill it to again. And the mountains, the forest, the place at the base of the spine. There is a black striped coho at the creek head: dream the coho leaping with his muscular urge out of the water. Silver and red-sided he turns, uncaught, uneaten, until the brown bear reaches the bank; the coho has returned to his origins from his exile at sea when the bear grabs him from the water; coho blood on the long claws. And in the bear mouth, the glassy, now unseeing fish eyes of the old salmon—who only moments ago glared, enraged and exalted, as he furiously swam homeward with his white clouds of spermatozoa tucked into his flesh in search of the redds of orange, newly deposited eye-eggs he could fertilize—have transformed.

NOW SHE HAS FALLEN ASLEEP. Now she is no longer in the brick house; she is moving toward the lighthouse and just before she arrives, she turns and heads toward the stairs of a hidden bunker whose concrete grey steel structure was built in 1941 by the US ARMY CORPS OF ENGINEERS as first defense against invaders. The steel railings of the stairwell have rusted through since that time and from a distance look like long red dashes suspended in midair. Several tall Monterey pines stand just beyond the fortification (their forms sculpted by the winter storms and gales so that the gnarled trunks tilt at an angle and the wide branches sweep outward toward the sea like arms extended in welcome). There is a white square sign on a concrete wall at the top of the stairway and large black letters painted onto it; the place is called THOMAS VICARS and who can say what for? She does not know to whom this sign might refer—is it a coded message or secret name for the travelers who close their eyes in G68 and find themselves walking along the below-ground hallway of the army bunker east of the lighthouse? Here there are ten underground rooms and each door is made of heavy stone. But she is stronger than ten men here and she pushes the door open easily; it is unnumbered, unglyphed, yet she knows with certainty which room is hers. Inside of the room it is black and in this blackness—which is not absence or presence, neither hot nor stinks nor joy nor love, but not either death—she begins.

She sees now, for her eyes have adjusted to the dimness, that there are no windows and there is a metal cot and there is a rickety wooden table and a solitary beaten metal folding chair. Perhaps there are sheets on the thin mattress. A pillow made of synthetic fibers, a woolen blanket. There is no language inside of the room; there are objects: the metal cot, the white bed sheets, a pillow and blanket, a small rickety wooden table, a metal folding chair. A light bulb hangs from the ceiling wire; it is not illuminated until she turns a switch and it now dimly, yet harshly lights the room. She lies on the bare mattress, for although her imagination made the bed into a sheeted and blanketed bed, it is not. She looks up at the ceiling and the lock in the door has shut loudly and she waits. She is a woman in her late forties, and she now therefore understands that she will live but a short time on the earth like all the earth's animals. She could be from any metropolis. She could speak in many decipherable tongues. As it is, she comes from a country where progress arrived like a light-up toy (as if a dream) in 1918. She is a cosmopolitan: a lonely, anxious, violent creature.

# FIVE

# THE NEW CITY

SHE WALKS IN THE NEW desert city. She seeks love and she seeks to arrive at the mountains in the distance (yet the further she walks, the farther they recede). She seeks a center of the place and authochthonous noises. In this new desert city, she is the only walker because it is too hot outside for pedestrians (106° Fahrenheit) and because this city was designed for the dimensions of the automobile and not to the scale of a man. There are ten-lane roads and huge concrete overpasses; high concrete walls surround the houses and driveways and parking lots. To move out, one must travel inside vehicles that move men and goods and despoil the air, the earth, the birded, sandy landscape. Colorful, loud cars rush by her (green, orange, yellow, grey, blue, and white hulls) and their closed-up, shut-off, black-tinted windows look to her like dead, scornful eyes. She is lonely as she walks because the automobile causes feelings of dissolution and separateness. She heads toward the tallest peak in the far distance; it recedes even as she wishes that it would advance.

She is on a concrete sidewalk now on a long wide street but it is empty of traffic and a wall ten stories high to her left shields homes, cars, and fescue grasses from her view and to her right, on the other side of the long street, another high wall shields the same model houses, automobiles, and lawns. She continues walking for she believes, for some reason, she might have a real adventure. She then passes an old Western-style corral and sees a blind horse inside of it; a tall chain-link fence separates her from the animal. The blind horse approaches her and tells her that this is a dead-end street. Behind the horse, next to the old corral, she sees an enormous ditch filled with brackish water and hundreds of chickens, geese, turkeys, rabbits, and swans walking around it in circles. They now tumble toward the fence, squawking loudly, screaming something in their languages which she cannot decipher. She continues walking and dozens of feral dogs begin to run back and forth along an adjacent chain-link fence, barking loudly and baring their teeth, and she would only like to reach Mount Ararat in the unreachable country. A cloud collects like a veil around the peak of that sacred mountain, and she has moved past the domesticated animals, she has left the walled corridor behind, and she now steps onto a concrete overpass. Hundreds of colorful vehicles with their opaque glass now rush past her and there is no animal or plant life she can see. The noise from the cars and the noises of the helicopters and aeroplanes in the machined sky above her fill the air with their din and strip her naked (for although her body remains clothed, her soul is bared, she thinks, by this onslaught to her ear). There is another immense chain-link fence at her right to shield her from a tragic fall onto the freeway below and she looks down through it and sees what she expected: her own grief, isolation, and losses (of quiet, of natural noises, of ease inside the soft center at her belly). She sees an artificial sluice: it is as wide as the widest portion of the old rivers in the old world and of undammed rivers in the new: perhaps a thousand men standing with their hands outstretched could not span it. Tens of thousands of cars rush down (and up) this unnatural causeway in the new desert city; they stream beneath her in either direction along the dozens of lanes made for their fast moving-along. The clamor is tremendous, ugly, and the concrete immensity of it: the latest and largest freeway takes people to where it is that they would like to go, which is nowhere, she thinks, this is the end; she has reached the apogee of the city.

She is sickened (at heart) by what she sees all around her, yet even so, standing in the immense heat amidst the cacophonous noise of the overpass, she thinks how much she would like a man (or a woman) to remove her clothes with her. Even here, I wish that I could make love a little bit before I reach the other side and soften myself with him before the mountain's retreating glare, before the torment of the fast machines, lie with her beneath the cloudless, light-blue sky, white-strong sun, and the black cosmos I can't see beyond it.

## NEW LOVE III

NOW SHE KNOWS THE SHAPE and size of his cock for he has placed it inside her body. Now she has seen his eyes in the morning when he awakened and they are a whiter speckled blue. Now she can see his bare feet, a blackened toenail. He has run his hands up her back, he has smiled into her mouth, he has slept and she could not sleep, listened to him breathe sleep-breaths and she thought about many things (her other lovers, her children) and of herself in the middle of the road of her life, and it is arduous, she is afraid, and there are many sacrifices yet to be made. And she could fall down into love with a man who, when she sees him, she must touch with her fingers, her elbows, her palms, the hair-stopped nape, to halt the terror which seeing and coming near him causes. The terror is there and the touch of his body abrades it violently, like an electric shock. And she is his loving, open-mouthed (she bares her neck for his slaughter) supplicant below the constellation of The Water-Pourer. Mouth agape.

(And he? He takes her hand and gently places it onto his cock.)

# COHOS

THE COHOS ARRIVE TO SPAWN in the creek that curves behind the underground bathhouse. This is the fall season when the
nights lengthen and the salmon return to their natal stream beds.
Migrating sandhill cranes pass overhead in sundry Vs and fill the
air with their ten-million-year-old song; it descends into the forest,
into human and non-human ears, and plays a while even after the
primordial birds have departed. Thousands more take their singing
place today after a break in the weather allows the resumption of
their southward winter journey and they animate the sky.

The once-silver female coho, now black-striped and putrefying,
has made the hundred-mile journey back home. She begins to thrash
a hole in the creek bed with her tail to deposit her orange eggs there.
And the male who has awaited his three-year return returns, and
afterwards unwithholds his cloud of white sperm upon them. The
female excavates another redd and a third in the shallow, gravelly
waters, and the male follows after her assiduously to release his milt
onto the translucent black-eyed orange eggs. These eyes gaze silently
into the cold, clear northern waters toward their futures.

The old male soon drifts away to his dying: his open-mouthed
beak, his disintegrating red lateral stripes and green back. The female

rests alongside the baskets of her progeny until the current also takes her. The eggs glow brightly in the grey gravel, stare darkly at the rotting corpses of mothers and paternal flesh around them. They alight eventually onto the creek in gleaming silver swimming patterns toward, in two years' time, the immutable and colder sea only to return again, today they returned as the sandhill cranes flew overhead, home to a shallow, cold northern decomposition and rebirth.

# DREAMING

IN THAT INSTANT YOU UNDERSTAND everything, as if you have understood the ancient, sacred text of a dead language. The closing of eyes leads you down, as into a steep vertical tunnel, or into the depths of a vast sea, and you know all of the laws; you comprehend the old symbols; the oracles at Delphi, Gryneium, and Clarus become apparent and golden-sided in your hands. It is all laid out before you, clear and comprehensible, and awaits you eagerly, like a new lover. When you open your eyes, it is gone. In reality, it was lost even before you opened them, diminished as you ascended inside the elevator, walked down the giant's laddered spine to returned upward to see the night sky once more. Your knowing had vanished before you looked back and Eurydice was rebanished for the length of another eternity.

THE MAN LEAVES HOME AT his wife's request and drives to the marketplace to purchase some food items for the morrow and this evening's meal. He was sent for milk and pasteurized cheeses, preserved meats, and sweet, salty snacks for their children's school lunches. He now wanders along the supermarket aisles and the food is boxes and beautiful and smiles at him from the brightly lighted shelves. They invite him to ease into their promise (of happiness and good health and order). He puts things into his cart, both the things that his wife requested and other attractively packaged, like Christmas gifts, colorful foods: there are yellow boxed crackers, glowing bags of potato chips, red and orange jams, cerulean tins of sardines, brown bottles of brown sauces, golden yellow and green pickles.

The man now peruses the SUGAR AND VINEGAR OILS aisle. He concentrates on his purchases; his face is closed and set, as if a mask. If a fellow shopper were to speak to him he would smile (with straightened, white teeth), notlisten, and reply curtly using the routine, polite phrases of the mistrustful middle-class citydweller so that he could quickly move from the speaker back to the alluring products around him. A young, provocatively dressed woman could catch his eye and although he might feel a sharp sexual urge, disdain would swiftly follow on its heels (for the slutty girl) and with his sex partly engorged he would turn away, back to the cardboard boxes and loud advertisements calling to him to own things.

So how is it then that in this state of mind a stranger approaches the man and speaks to him of a house on a moor which then becomes an offer to visit and the offer which the man does not refuse? The stranger says—*Dear Sir*—and no one employs this formal term of address any longer—*May I help you?*

Perhaps it was the genuine, kind regard of the stranger as he spoke to the man. Or perhaps it was because after the man slipped on an oil spot and lost his balance and fell onto the black-and-white checkered floor of the supermarket and the foods and fluorescent lights glared down at him and reproached him and his clumsy shameful manner (*do you stink? do you shit and piss? will you, do you even now, decay and weaken, lose color with age?*), the stranger had gently leaned down toward him and (for reasons the man himself could not understand) evoked in him a strong sensation, like a rap on the top of his head. Yet it was not injury, but something in the stranger's countenance because as the stranger lay his hand on the recumbent's shoulder and inquired after his wellbeing, the man looked into the dark aperture of the stranger's pupils and saw there unexpectedly the image of his mother who lived now in a convalescing home and whom he hardly visited, and then his father who died nearly a decade ago. And after, as if in a moving picture, the speckled blue robin's egg he found in the woods behind his house when he was five years old. And then he was sitting behind his father on a motorcycle as they traversed the low-lying hills outside of town and the wind was on them and sunlight and tall trees loomed above them and he laughed out loud in continuous whoops and aw-haws as he held his father tightly. His mother stood at the stove in the kitchen with her old dark hair, old memories intact (*My son*, she said, *where did you go?*) sautéing onions in butter that he could smell as he passed by her on the way to his bedroom from the garden with the natural blue treasure held gently in his palm; there would be rice pilaf (his favorite) for the evening meal.

He said nothing in response to the stranger's question, for he had been sobbing on the black-and-white checkered floor and snot dripped from his chin onto his shirt and he couldn't yet catch his breath or speak. His eyes had become smaller and redder and blind; the wrinkles tightened across the aging skin of his face; the two furrows between his eyes were now deep sluices. He eventually uttered an affirmative, but he knew it was not the fall or his shame and loneliness in his marriage and disillusionment with his life or the losses that compelled him, albeit nervous and afraid, to go to the brick house, to a place, the stranger said, where he could rest and restore himself.

Six days later he received the call and the day following drove to the airport (the lies to his wife about business travel because although he had decided to visit the brick house, he couldn't adequately articulate his reasons to anyone, certainly not his spouse with whom he shared an agreed-upon vision of the world and state of things, busyness, obligations, historical timelines, and plans). He was fully aware as he boarded the aeroplane, however, that he went to the brick house not because of what the stranger had said to him or how the stranger had looked (the unmask of his visage) and not because of something that had lowered his defenses or breached them or slid along the interstitial byways and roads of his ideas, causing a rupture of some kind. His was a pure, non-rational action without explicable cause and effect.

# SIX

# NEW LOVE IV

HER FATHER ARRIVES TO HER home for a visit and she is afraid (again). He takes her down the latent corridors of her memory not with words, but via his paternal timbre: his familiar voice tones do it. He speaks and she is the young girl inside her childhood bedroom and he is fast approaching. His shod feet move across the wooden floorboards toward her room where, upon arriving, he will berate her, beat her, tell her that she is not right, that she oughtn't to do that, that why isn't she more and more like this: a goodgirl.

She drives across the large bay to visit the new lover after the father (and the Father) depart on an aeroplane. She is, perchance, aggrieved. There is something which she cannot name, which she will, for lack of a precise term, call *her sorrow*. For? For the father because the Father (like a ghost encased in sound) still walks loudly down the hallway toward her bedroom, black belt tucked into his large avenging hands (the Giant, the Demon) when the father arrives for a visit from the East Coast.

She walks into the new lover's home. He is beautiful today, she thinks. He is fully clothed and he smiles to see her, washes dishes in the kitchen with a dark, wetted cloth. *I must attend these,* he says. She stands by his side awkwardly; she waits, thinks: Father is walking down the rough lining of my spine. He is hunting his daughter. She has not brought a spade or mallet, but she decides she will destroy Him tonight. She moves closer to the new lover; he cleans plates, bowls, and cups in his bright-lighted kitchen. She puts her hand onto his back; she puts her hand onto his ass. She kisses him. She turns him; she is killing. He washes and cleans and turns from her, then turns back to her and asks her if she is hungry. *You are hungry, I can see it*, he says. She presses her body into his body; she feels his arousal. He is a stranger to her; in reality, his heart is another dark room. Inside the long corridor of her spine, meanwhile, the Father's steps sound like heavy stones thrown against a hardwood floor.

The new lover lifts up the girl and she wraps her arms and legs around his torso and he walks them to his bedroom. The hallway is long and brightly lit and the length of the wooden floors are covered in a red Persian carpet that muffles his footsteps. She is now lying on her back where he has placed her onto his large bed. There is no speech; there are loud bodies, his loud breathing (her own breath invisible and silent to her). He shuts his eyelids if she looks too closely into his hiding, speckled blue, scared eyes: he is afraid; she frightens him (or the Father frightens him? or the banshee each girl carries at the base of the spine does it?) There are movements; there is the friction of longing and two bodies and the newness of the new lovers' bodies. They are naked; he has removed her dress; he has removed his shirt, his trousers. She knows that she will not have an orgasm with him tonight; she is not aroused, she thinks, though her sex is wet, soft, and blood-filled red like the dark red of the Persian carpet in the hallway. She looks at him; he does not look at her. You are beautiful, she says inside of herself, for she sees the beauty of the man: his arms, his chest, and the curve of muscle, and mostly it is the large blood-filled cock which she delights in. The joy of the aroused sex she now takes into her hands. And long before he fucks her, she wets her fingertips with the smallest amount of his fluids which emerged and will emerge fully into the latex encasing his cock inside of her cunt half an hour from now when he ejaculates.

Afterwards she tells him that he is beautiful. He turns from her; *No*, he says, *I don't feel like that. Tell me*, she says, *that I am beautiful also*. And the new lover turns back to the beloved, looks at her for a moment; he has returned to his fear again now that he is unaroused as if returning to the hidden paths which bordered his childhood home; his trepidation and caution is familiar and reminds him of that old place. *When I saw you tonight*, he says, *I thought that you looked good*.

By accident later that night, after they have taken a meal at a roadside restaurant and they are sitting and waiting to pay their bill, she will give him a kiss, and then by violent accident she will bite his bottom lip and see that she has made him bleed. He complains to her of it, turns from her and takes money from his wallet. She is mortified, ashamed, sullen and looks toward the back of the restaurant and sees how the Father laughs from a dark corner at His ashamed and ill-begotten (ill-starred, she wonders, in love?) daughter.

She leaves her new lover's apartment later in the night. He does not escort her to her car on the deserted city street. I don't love you, she says inside of herself: I won't. I'll not talk to you again, she thinks. (The Father laughs; he is delighted. He jumps up and down with glee like any spiteful child who takes great pleasure when another falls down and bloodies her knee.)

She drives toward the cantilever bridge that connects the new lover's city to hers and a policeman stops her and issues a speeding ticket because, he says, she has exceeded the limits. *I haven't*, she says.

The new beloved is a liar; the new beloved feels terror at the outset. *Please*, she said to the new lover: *tell me your name. One who is like god?* he said.

# WATER

*As to my heavy sins, I remember one most vividly:*
*How, one day, walking a forest path along a stream,*
*I pushed a rock down onto a water snake coiled in the grass.*
*And what I have met with in life was the just punishment*
*Which reaches, sooner or later, everyone who breaks a taboo.*

—Czeslaw Milosz, "Bypassing Rue Descartes"

THE EARTH IS DRY AND sparsely covered in creosote, saguaro, mesquite, and the baked sand of the semi-arid plains. The horizon stretches far off into the flat distance; there are not mountains, just this plate and the dried browns, tans, grey-green hues of the earth; the spiny, silvery plants; the quick moving, heat-seeking lizards. She hears a loud sound from belowground and she would like to find a companion (she is alone here) because after she hears the subterranean boom, the earth begins to crack and long, jagged crevices to appear and fan out (like spindly black spider legs) and she wants to know for what reason and to share her trepidation.

From the invisible center, seeping up and out of the monstrous fissures, the blue, clean, cold waters of melted ice caps, of the lake in paradise, now rush forth. It is a blue which seems too blue for itself even, made of mineral devotion and it looks like something pure and young and free, and never before seen on the surface of the earth. The girl is happy to see the beauty of the bright water, and worried that some damage was done by the explosion in the invisible center, that there will be more eruptions, more black chasms that fill with the waters of the last earthly aquifer. And something else emerges alongside the girl's admiration and misgivings; it has no designation in language (yet) but moves powerfully nonetheless, like the new waters, rushes forth inside her.

# THE LAYSAN ALBATROSS

THE ATOLL LIES ON THE far outer edges of the subtropical gyre, one thousand miles from the island in the Pacific, and here no man resides. It looks like paradise on the atoll. See the fishes. See no men. See the clear, warm waters and coral reefs. The Laysan albatrosses wing in wide-wingèd formations. Petrels, noddies, terns, plovers, and sandpipers live here. Hear their constant calls, their ruckus; the shit smell of white-yellow guano all round; the nests and chicks and the perpetual energetic movements of flight, of landings. There is a monk seal who calls out to his mate near the blue lagoon; the sky above is another bright white-blue. There is life and increase inside of these images. Don't see the military barracks or lead paint. The concrete bunker or metal girdings. You are not in the brick house; you are not in the underground bunker. You don't know of the atoll's existence—of a battle fought here in 1941 with loud contaminating enemy forces. Of runways, of a gymnasium, of military might, and spilled petrol on the sandy inlets. You decide, therefore, to take a stroll. You are walking along the loud beach where there are no men except for you walking and there is the ruckus bird shit smell everywhere. You can, if you'd like, see the albatross flying above your head; the albatross does not hang about the mariner's neck as he did in the old poem, rather it is the traveler who hangs upon the bird's brow, the bird's beak, inside of its filled-to belly. With what is the albatross's belly filled to? Walking, you can't see it: red cigarette lighter, yellow bottle cap, a child's miniature toy soldier. The bird went to the subtropical gyre in search of food—found cap, lighter, a miniature toy soldier—which it now gives to its offspring who sits waiting patiently here on the atoll. See the nests in the grasses. One chick waits inside each nest for its food while the wide-wingèd birds travel across the North Pacific gyre, hunt, discover delicious colored feasts to fill up their bellies heavily as if with meat stones. Birds return to the atoll as you walk along the grasses, depart, now you see a bird carcass, now you bend down. Each wide wing of this wide-wingèd bird body is spread out upon the sand, as if a small Christ. The bones of the bird are like sticks upon the grass; some other creature has already picked the meat clean; the bacteria, the flies have done their flesh-cleaning work also, so that there are feathers, there are bones, there is the cross formation the wings make upon the earth. And the noise of birds is loud all around you and the shit smell and unheeding you pluck the blackest albatross feather for your brow, take up a cigarette lighter, a red bottle cap from the exposed guts of the wild dead creature, for these remained on the grasses from the meal hunted from the North Pacific gyre which was this beast's demise: the chick died with a filled-up (heavy like stones), unnourished belly. And the plastic meal persists long afterwards, and you toss the three items of trash back into the sea until another bird—petrel or sandpiper—takes it for its colorful dinner with delight, its end bright and attractive upon the gleaming sea waters, upon the shores and grasses of the atoll. The birds feed from the gyre, from your own distant city. You feed the albatross (eventually) with the red plastic stick you used to dissolve the sugar into your coffee this morning (the lighters, the caps, the bags, the wraps, the hulls and covers and containers and toys you purchased) in your city. Pick up a bright stick and stir your hot beverage; toss it away. And away it goes until some of it will be taken into the sea, ingested by the sea animals and birds and arrive to this atoll in the belly of a Laysan albatross one thousand miles from the island in the Pacific, in the middle of nowhere (and the plastic things become smaller and smaller, until, eventually, you too will eat your detritus in the meat of the fish for your dinner in the tiniest polymers residing there) so the world itself falls down upon the island: yellows blues greens and reds from America from Asia from the barges and potent refrains of progress and convenience.

# THE END OF THE LOVE AFFAIR II

THE BELOVED LIES NAKED AND spraddle-legged on the bed. The lover is between her legs and dips his head toward her sex. *Wait*, she says. The beloved places her hand inside of her sex and, removing three fingers, sees they are covered in her menstrual blood. *I'm bleeding*, she says. Her blood flows onto the bed sheets. The lover says that he isn't bothered and he puts his mouth to her sexual mouth and begins to pleasure her; to eat her. *You have changed water into blood*, he says. The lover moves his bloody clean mouth to her breast and sucks her large nipple. *Into milk.*

He leaves a wide red mark on her areola.

The beloved, who had felt ashamed and ill at ease, now feels reassured about their future.

# THE VISIBLE HIDDEN AWAY GODS II

*Like you, he was irreverent to the god. That's why the god linked you and him together in the same disaster, thus destroying the house.*
          —Euripides, *Bacchae*

THE OLD MAN SITS WITH his brother at the dining table and eats his dinner from a tin can. Soon he sees each thing twoly. Two brothers in front of him, two wives in the kitchen, two cans of beer, two cans of meat on two tables. The twos then become ones again but ones he can no longer distinguish; they are like blurred charcoal drawings: the wife, the can, the beer, the brother, the table no longer have sharp lines or limits. Then his feet lose all feeling, his tongue goes numb, and his mouth makes slurred words like his eyes make blurred images. The eyelids begin to close and then for the closure he cannot see. His mouth opens and his tongue pushes out and from his stomach the bile comes forth and he has vomited onto his trousers and shoes and the table. He stands and then he cannot stand; he is sitting again and then he cannot sit; the muscles of the body quickly remove themselves from any kind of response and he lies like a stranded sea animal on the edge of his outer-banks dining room. He is losing the movement of his fingers; now the lungs begin to undo their up and back movements; the liver does not circulate; the spleen is white and becoming fatter. The can of meat stares at him from the table. The small animals that were inside of the can, brought from abroad as an uninvited souvenir, smile congenially; happily they trip around his bloodstream like girls skipping down a lane. The small animals lived in the dark, unoxygenated earth; the small animals traveled a long distance; the small animals ate his nerve endings like he ate the canned meat.

The ambulance rushes him to the hospital. His wife holds his unfeeling hand, touches the unfeeling eyes; machines push his lungs open and closed. With each machined breath, there is oxygen moving into the blood and waste moving out of his mouth. He is traveling in the river of his own blood; he is having the dream about the man who tries to run and cannot run. The machines push his lungs as Sisyphus pushed the giant boulder up the mountain (only to see it fall down again). Then he is running very quickly, as if he were flying almost, for he has awakened on a football field in America and he is the football star and the game is mid-play and he sees in the crowd of onlookers how his mother and father hold their hands up into the air in the form of the conquering V. His wife is happy; his brother is relieved. He is V.

# RAIN

THE RAINS HAVE FINALLY RETURNED and the man thinks about his garden and of how contented the plants will now be, for he did not water them during the months of drought and they drooped and swagged and began to lose their dark green foliage to lighter, unhappier greens, browns. The man understands, for he is a scientist, what causes rainfall, but he doesn't understand (for he is not a metaphysician) the cause of causes.

The rain abates and the man goes into the garden and sees how the bushes and groundcover and tree leaves are greener-looking already. He looks up at the sky and three hawks pass overhead in sweet unbridled pattern. He has studied patterns for many years. He has read many textbooks and scientific reports and he knows many things, but not this: what makes the plant strike up its leaves in such chlorophylled joy? What holds the molecules of his own body together and the blue planet in spinning, starry blackness?

The scientist and his garden dissolve into blackness. The rains begin again. Unabated continue.

*ARRIVE TO THE MOOR,* the stranger said to him in the market-place, *open the rosewood door, re-see things as they are.*

# SEVEN

## THE END OF THE LOVE AFFAIR III

FOR SOME REASON, SHE IS unable to walk. She sits in a wheelchair and she pushes herself around by turning the large wheels with her hands. She sees her lover's friend, R, inside a dining hall filled with many people. *Have you seen him?* she asks, and R says that he is at the other side of the fair. There are hundreds of people milling around inside the building and outside in the small suburban downtown area for today's festivities. She continues her journey in search of the lover (to ask his forgiveness? to relove him? to take him back and assure him of her relove?) She runs into another of her lover's friends and he directs her to take the bike path. Then she sees P and S and B and they tell her that yes, they have seen him, that she must continue up this incline and over to where the dancers are hosting a party, on the playground where the children are laughing, behind the Polynesian hut where the pig was set into the ground hours ago to cook slowly: there you'll find him. She pushes her chair up the hill and down, and she is outside and she is inside of ancient temples and she is on the concrete pathway lined with symmetrically planted palms and cut fescue grasses and each time that she arrives to a place, her lover has already departed. And she knows, suddenly, that she won't catch up with him by remaining in this wheelchair and so she stands and she realizes that she can walk, and that she can, in fact, run, and so she begins running and she is happy she is not paralyzed, or sick, or suffering acute low-back pain.

Then she is sitting at a table in a fine dining restaurant and her son (he is three years old again) sits on the floor beneath the white linen tablecloth hidden from view. She is talking to R about her plans for the future (without her lover) and somehow her son has put his tiny penis into her vagina and then he put his hands into her vagina and she feels that she is about to come very soon and she recalls how the lover made her orgasm wildly: his mouth to her sex, his tongue on her clitoris, his beautiful lips which brought her ecstasy day after day during their affair.

# THE OLD CITY

THEY ARE ON A SMALL skiff traveling down a large river through the forest and the evergreens rise tall and massive above them. The girl is with her guide and two strangers and as she stares up at the great stand of trees on the river's roadway, she suddenly understands to what and from where the city and its structures owe their forms.

She had had a dream of walled cities while she traveled along the ancient river into the ancient forest. And in that dream the skyscrapers rose taller than the great trees. And the people milled about in a frenzy: they mobbed the buildings, the roads, the airways and waterways. And there was burning metal when a helicopter detonated behind the sky, filling it thereby with hot broken steel and plastics; and there were more plastics in each thing; there were factories, machines, and conveyor belts; and people pushing and pulling, walking and running along the roads and sidewalks and stepping into automobiles and onto underground trains and boarding aeroplanes, fast motorboats, large ships. There were not other animals in this dream; there was not a gallery of trees or a wild river or black soil. The aquifer was emptied. The sky black-brown.

In the dream, a nightmare, the city was built where today the girl and her guide and the two strangers travel. So that she wonders:

will a city be built someday on the top of this forest and the river un-rivered (the waters removed); the forest unforested (the trees taken down); the songbirds, the hawks and rodents and large hunting and hunted megafauna destroyed and undone?

But she recalls how when she had awakened from that dream, she saw above her the verdant canopy and blue sky from where she lay on her back on the wet humus of the earth. And her guide, who slept beside her, had awakened soon thereafter and lifted her up and leaned her gently into the trunk of a wide evergreen, removed her skirt, she pulled up his shirt, and they made love against the old tree with skin pressed to skin to tree bark and afterwards she slept again and undreamed the new city beneath the green and blue dome of the old heavens.

# THE END OF THE LOVE AFFAIR IV

THE BELOVED HAS BEEN WORKING inside a building at her desk in a windowless cubicle since early in the morning. She is anxious to complete the tasks expected of her, and these tasks entail using her skills as an analyst and organizer of data. She packs up her belongings; the work day has ended, and she leaves the building and goes out onto the street. Everything is at first familiar as she begins to walk down the boulevard (cars pass by her, the facades of buildings slowly pass by her) except that the light outside is a dim orange and the sky itself a bright white. Soon, however, the architecture, the sidewalks, and the wide street begin to remind her of the city of her childhood, so that she wonders if this is no longer the city she lives in in reality. She passes several shops and seeks to confirm her location by the familiar name of a street. Finally, she reaches an intersection and a blue street sign with white letters, but the name on it is not one she recognizes, nor is it a word in her language, and she doesn't know how it has happened but somehow upon leaving her place of employment this evening she entered into another city (that resembles the city of her childhood) in another country and she is lost.

She continues her peregrination. She leaves the city center behind as the sun begins to set (although she cannot see its descending orange orb). There are no natural earth markers: not trees, birds, squirrels, or other city animals; or bushes or flowers; or a river; or the sea in the distance; or mountains which rise above her. There is the tarmac of the boulevard, the perfectly measured sidewalk adjacent to it, the new buildings one after the other that look like boxes and which are department stores and auto stores and a large pharmacy chain she has seen all over her country. In fact, the names of all of the stores are familiar company brands, but the light (orange) and sky (white) remain strange. She still carries her brown briefcase filled with useless (now) numbers and fractions of numbers and lists of things she must do; she has a wallet with her country's valueless money inside of it. Soon she enters a residential area and passes row upon row of two-story single-family homes that remind her of her parents' old house but she knows that that place no longer exists, as they do not either, for they have died already.

Long after dark she reaches the frontier, and there she meets an old couple playing poker inside a new casino. They offer her a meal (she dropped her briefcase and wallet miles ago) and they tell her that they can help her find her way. She climbs into their car in the hope of driving closer to the familiar in her memory.

# JOY

THERE IS—

The white light shines, notburns.

The feeling which moves out (like the tides [difficult, nay, impossible? to language without the comparison, and the comparison must be to wild things and places {the source of all reality}]: the tide moves in, the acorn barnacle opens its closed hatch, the six-fingered hand-mouth waves out, grabs, pulls in; the bear'd wood; a red-tailed hawk turning in circles on the rising thermal of the afternoon; the bald eagle preparing to hunt his prey from the spine-tip of the tallest hemlock; in a small skiff moving down Chatham Strait, the wide grey ancient mountains, the blue-bright glacier in the distance, the grey-blue waters pulling the souls and heavy organs of the captain of the skiff and his companion, the girl who traveled a long distance to arrive here, high unto the untreed pinnacle).

The newborn in the lap of the young mother, he suckles.

The new lovers, he reaches, she reaches, for the other's ancient hand, blindly, tentatively, inside of their radical mortality, the blue veins like cobras which crisscross the plains of each hand, the contained blood which reaches outward toward gnosis.

## NEW LOVE V

YOU HAVE RETURNED FROM A long sojourn abroad and you wait patiently at the side of the road. She crosses the street (traffic moving fast) to join you. You have opened your arms; you have smiled widely. She shyly turns her gaze, worried, wary; perhaps you are a demon? No, you have only smiled widely. You embrace her now, you whisper into her ear about carnival, the place you would like to take her tonight. You take her hand and you begin to walk through the streets of the city. See that she is beautiful. See that he is a centaur and puts her onto his back and they run with the cars beneath the concrete overpasses, through the tunnels, and across the bridges. She holds your horseneck tightly and you soon arrive to the festival entrance and buy two tickets, as to a ride, and enter this new world.

He is a man again, takes her hand. She is naked from the waist up and her breasts move from side to side as she walks. He guides her through the confusion. There is music playing in all four corners; there are thousands of people dressed in colorful costume; there are wild monkeys swinging from electric wires; sad, lonely intoxicated people; ecstatic dancers; brave, mad women; naked men swinging their cocks. There are green, bright lights (it is nighttime now); there are smiles larger than the human hand; there are people fucking; there are people looking for the people they can fuck with. And he touches her all the while, puts his hand onto the nape of her neck, rubs her back, does not release her as he leads her down into the cavern with the two-headed marionettes. He stays with her in the bedroom while she rouges her nipples. Then they are in the middle of a wide circle lighted all round not by electric lights but by stored sunlight glowing brightly now at midnight. They stand together naked and he pulls her toward him and places his hands on her back and ass, they dance inside of the circle, he pulls her closer and then pushes her back, other dancers push and pull at the two lovers, and it is awkward at the start of it, he pushing, she pulling, to find a rhythm where, finally, he and she, lover and beloved, move together easily along the cold current of the blue northern river as the female and male coho salmon swim upstream, the humpback whale travels toward warmer birthing waters in the south, the sandhill cranes fly overhead in cacophonous Vs. The lover pulls and she pushes until the sunlight is pushing down into her and into him and they are no longer the two new lovers: they are outside of history and their birth names; he is aroused and she is arousing him in the age-old game of seduction. She is wet; he can smell her cunt fluids. She turns to him and she turns away from him; he follows her. She follows him back.

Hours later, at dawn, they rest on clean woolen blankets and she will tell him the story of the Urartian queen who seduced the young king east of the Rhine with her stone letters. Of how she sent him invisible missives across the conquered and unconquered lands of East and West, across the past and into a future, beyond blood and clan. And of the house she traveled to once when she felt too lonely and desirous and without the old ways or the dead, and where, she says to him, *In a wood,* (Sitka spruce, western hemlock and yellow cedar, a short distance from the brick house) *I fell asleep and dreamed in an indecipherable and obsolete tongue, inside of an as yet unwritten book. And at the end of the story cycle?* he asks. *This one,* she replies as she cradles him gently in their lair, *is not for the angry blind son. For who then?* he says, as the sun lifts skyward.

# THE BRICK HOUSE

*Dreams are the guiding words of the soul.*

—C.G. Jung, *The Red Book*

THE CARETAKER CARES FOR THE material world. She drives the motor car; she provides the 6:15 a.m. breakfast, clean towels; she ensures hot water. But who carries the dreamer on his back down the demon's spine, out of the seventh room of the long and dimly lit hallway, upward toward starlight? Who guides her gently along the path?

The dreamer descends and ascends alone. He turns; his own knowledge; her own understanding. Beyond information and conclusive evidence and the borders of clarity and causes, nearer the invisible breaths, silence on the edges of speech, the blood's perpetual whisperings in signs and images.

Hold the heart of the shriveled beast in your hand—this is your heart also. Take money and reason and heaps of data and toss them into the river (alongside the white plastic jugs of petrochemicals, amidst the colorful polyethylene bags). The strangest dream was the one you dreamed before you arrived: of lonely, unnatural men.

Move onto the moor, into the house, down the hallway with the seven doors (the seven-headed dragon, the thirteen-eyed beast); each door leads into a room and inside of this room there is an inside door; open it: you are now at the center of the heptagon, inside the mystery of the edifice, beyond the symbol, all the doors and all the dreams, each strange and quotidian form, lead here: listen to the rush at the back of your mind.

For the dreams are given to the man, given to the woman: the woods, the old temples, the old verse, the brick house, *The Brick House,* the immanent world, palpable, the high mountain of Ararat, exact and holy, that when climbed once more leads outward as if into a continuously murmuring sea.

*Lo duca e io per quel cammino ascoso*
*intrammo a ritornar nel chiaro mondo;*
*e sanza cura aver d'alcun riposo,*
*salimmo sù, el primo e io secondo,*
*tanto chi'i'vidi de le cose belle*
*che porta 'l ciel, per un pertugio tondo.*
*E quindi uscimmo a riveder le stelle.*

—Dante, *Inferno*

*PERHAPS YOU THOUGHT THIS WAS notreal*, the caretaker says;
she scratches her fat belly, blows her nose loudly into a cloth handker-
chief. These dream-made black-and-white paper dilapidated buildings.
*You see, it was not the brick house that called to you but you who made*
*and called to it*, and then she turns from him, a man in his forties, a
medical doctor, an engineer and store clerk, a plumber and barman,
a big boss or vagabond, a businessman, and she commands him to
put his black valise on the floor and to remove his clothes. He does so
quickly. *Lie down*, she says, and he has lain his body on the small bed
in R97, and she removes her shirt her trousers and she climbs onto
him; she is fat, unseemly, her teeth now, he can see, are broken in
places and her breath smells of alcohol and decay. She laughs into his
face and kisses him deeply, puts her green and yellow tongue into his
mouth, and he has never been more aroused than he is right now. He
pushes her off of him to push her down below his body; she is laughing like a young, delighted nubile girl, and he can smell her diseased,

putrid earthy cunt and then, entering her (she is wet and tight and holds him), he is out of the brick house, has passed by the lighthouse, out of the underground bunker, out of the promontory; he is flying; he is the half-albatross half-man with his long cock hanging down toward the earth and his wide-wingèd arms taking him toward the light of the moon over the vast seas beyond the islands and outside of the weather into the black-light air, behind Pegasus and Andromeda and toward the Pleiades, and what he has always known in his small cosmic human heart.

*He went to the house, he said, when the despair was too much for him.*

—Yasunari Kawabata, *House of the Sleeping Beauties*

*After death it's to reality I'll go. For the time being it's a dream. A fateful dream. But afterwards—afterwards everything is real.*

—Clarice Lispector, *Soulstorm*

# ENDNOTES

1. Epigraph: "Ah, ye admonitions and warnings!…" Herman Melville, *Moby Dick* (Boston: C.H. Simonds Company, 1922) 158.

2. Epigraph: "He understood that modeling …" Jorge Luis Borges, "The Circular Ruins," *Ficciones* (New York: Grove Press, 1962) 59.

3. Epigraph: "It is not outside…" Meister Eckhart as cited in C.G. Jung, *Dreams* (New Jersey: Princeton University Press, Bollingen Series: 1974) 176.

4. "He who has not yet killed…" As cited in Joseph Campbell, *The Inner Reaches of Outer Space* (New York: Alfred Van Der Marck Editions, 1986) 13.

5. "Before such an ell-embracing…" Roberto Calasso, *Literature and the Gods* (New York: Vintage, 2001) 56.

6. "Vocatus atque non vocatus…" Desiderius Erasmus, *Adagia*, attributed to Delphic Oracle and carved over the door of C.G. Jung's house, as cited in Edward Armstrong Bennet, *Meetings with Jung* (Einsiedeln, Switzerland: Daimon Verlad, 2012) 65.

7. "Seeing things as separate…" Adi Shankara as cited in Eknath Easwaran and Michael N. Nagler, *The Upanishads: The Classics of Indian Spirituality* (Canada: The Blue Mountain Center of Meditation, 2007) 340.

8. "The map of Babylon…" Mircea Eliade, *The Myth of the Eternal Return or, Cosmos and History* (New Jersey: Princeton University Press, Bollingen Series XLVI, 1954) 10.

9. "You do not know…" Euripides, *The Bacchae*, *Euripides V* (Chicago: University of Chicago Press, 1959) 177.

10. "As to my heavy sins…" Czeslaw Milosz, *The Witness of Poetry*, (Cambridge: Harvard University Press, 1983) 9.

11. "Like you, he was irreverent…" Euripides, 185.

12. "Dreams are the guiding…" C.G. Jung, *The Red Book* (New York: W.W. Norton & Company, 2009) 233.

13. "Lo duca e io per quell cammino…" [My leader and I entered on that hidden road to return into the bright world; and caring not for any rest, we climbed up, he first and I second, so far that through a round opening I saw some of the beautiful things that Heaven bears; and thence we issued forth to see again the stars.] Dante Alighieri, *The Divine Comedy, Inferno* (New Jersey: Princeton University Press, Bollingen Series LXXX, 1970) 368.

14. "He went to the house…" Yasunari Kawabta, *House of the Sleeping Beauties* (Tokyo: Kodansha International, 1980) 22.

15. "After death…" Clarice Lispector, *Soulstorm* (New York: New Directions, 1989) 146.

## ABOUT THE AUTHOR

Micheline Aharonian Marcom was born in Dhahran, Saudi Arabia and raised in Los Angeles. She has published five novels, including a trilogy of books about the Armenian genocide and its aftermath in the twentieth century. She has received fellowships and awards from the Lannan Foundation, the Whiting Foundation, and the US Artists' Foundation. Marcom is also the founder of a digital, public arts storytelling project documenting the stories of Central American refugees: www.newamericanstoryproject.org. She teaches Creative Writing at Mills College and Goddard College.

## ABOUT THE ARTIST

Fowzia Karimi has a background in Visual Arts and Biology. She has an MFA in Creative Writing from Mills College. In her work, she combines the written and visual arts to tell stories. She was a recipient of The Rona Jaffe Foundation Writers' Award in 2011. She lives in Texas.

## ACKNOWLEDGMENTS

This book was a long time in the making. Many thank yous for reading along the way to: Carolina De Robertis, Pamela Harris, Joel Tomfohr, Peter Maravelis, and the staff, faculty, and students of the Goddard College MFA-WA.

And to the wonderful women of Awst: Tatiana Ryckman and her thoughtful insights; Emily Roberts and her sharp eye; LK James for the unity of the whole; and Wendy M. Walker who keeps it all together—were it not for you this book would still be a dream.